KILLING THE MATH

KILLING THE MATH

Joey Truman

Whiskey Tit
NYC & VT

If you intend to steal any or all parts of this book, steal it with cun- ning and grace. And maybe even tell us how you intend to use it.

Cover art by Jack Warren. Book design by Michael Jung.

This book was produced using PressBooks.com, and PDF rendering was done by PrinceXML.

Preface

I started writing this book two weeks after I finished *Postal Child*. I don't know why. I had always planned on writing it when I was too old to care and everybody in the book was dead. But I wrote it. I wrote it pretty quick. I now realize why. I used to have a friend named Gandalf, god bless his fucking soul, when he was alive he never showered regularly, but when he did he called it a purging, he would just build up all the gross and terrible things that human beings collect for weeks on end, and then when he couldn't take it anymore he would hop in the shower and purge. And then, just like that, he would be back to normal, clean as a fucking whistle.

Killing The Math is a purge of sorts. Whatever horrible and wretched things I had collected on my body and my soul while writing *Postal Child* came sloughing off because of writing this book. And because of this, *Killing The Math* wouldn't exist without *Postal Child*.

But I am lucky, I have somebody in my life that is willing to listen to this rhetoric and find it interesting enough to use the resources they have and put these thoughts out into the berth. By somebody I mean Whiskey Tit, and more specifically The Publisher.

And because of this luck we can look at these two books side to side, one guy goes up, and the other guy goes down.

When I wrote both of these books the viewpoint was very simple. I had no trouble imagining myself as a thirteen year old boy getting the shit kicked out of himself while being resilient just the same, and I had no trouble imagining myself as a sixteen year old boy growing up in Wyoming, because that is what I did. One mentally and one physically.

But there is a cross-over so I will finally get to my point:

Postal Child is a work of pure fiction. The only truth to it is that I did indeed see a homeless man pushing a mail cart around with bags of trash in it while wearing a postal service uniform.

Killing The Math, however, is a farce, the people exist, that is true, and the places exists, and most of the actions exists, but what really happened, I don't know. I have a horrible memory, but I also have an acute memory. I can remember the smell you make when you shift on a chair, but I won't remember the twenty minute conversation we have afterwards.

What I mean is, don't take any of this personally, it's just the story of a boy growing up in a horrible place wishing for something more. I would change the names, but what's the point, you're the only one who knows who that person is.

I didn't write this story, the story wrote itself.

Blame the story, not me.

—JOEY TRUMAN

Acknowledgements

A very Special Thanks to:

Miette Gillette
Michael Jung
Jack Warren
Ariana Smart Truman
James Oseland

To George: you are my daughter. Good luck.

Killing The Math

It was an exercise in courage. That's what he had called it. Another friend would call it that too, but that would be years later and he would be referring to riding his bike down a hill with his eyes closed. This was different. We were standing on top of Boysen Dam looking down into the reservoir. It was night. It had to be. Otherwise we couldn't be where we were standing. Had it been daylight, the view would knock your socks off. Boysen Reservoir stretched out in front of us for some twenty miles, and behind us was the canyon. The Wind River canyon.

The dam was off limits. What we were doing was illegal. We had ditched the car on the side of the highway and walked in. Jumping a fence. Using only moonlight. My friend got there first. He was smoking a cigarette, looking down. We had had to navigate some boulders before we got to where he was standing. There was a giant concrete slab that dropped vertically into the water. Maybe sixty feet.

The summer had been an odd one for this part of Wyoming. It had rained enough that the farmers didn't need as much water from the canals, and the spring thaw hadn't overfilled the reservoir, so the dam was essentially closed. The gates, that is. So the danger of being sucked into a violent eddy and spit out the other side to our immediate deaths was minute.

The three of us stood there looking down. Standing on the edge of the giant concrete slab. My friend threw his cigarette butt into the air. We counted five seconds before it hit the water. But that was a cigarette butt. The real concern was the depth of the water and how to land. Stay as vertical as you can, and point your toes. And the water must be high enough. How much depth do you need? Twenty feet? At most. I guess.

The three of us took off our shoes and stripped to our underwear. It was decided it would be smart to put our shoes back on. After we did this we stood there on the giant concrete slab again. This time almost naked. Our bright white bodies reflecting moonlight.

– Don't be a pussy! It's an exercise in courage. –

I couldn't tell you why I went first. I asked for a cigarette. I smoked it looking down. Thinking. Thinking. I finished the cigarette and threw it down. Something about that action changed something. Fuck it, I said, and just like that I was falling and falling and falling.

Normally when you jump off things into water, by the time you realize you had leapt you've hit the water. Not this time. At first I braced for impact, but I was still falling, so I relaxed, but then I seized up again. I forgot to point my toes. When I hit the water my feet tore through the soles of my shoes causing my legs to go behind my body and therefore smacking my face against the water. I must have turned my head because my nose was unharmed. How far down I went into the water is unclear, but it was far enough that as I was swimming to the surface I was afraid I might run out of air. But when I breeched, it was pure glory. I screamed. I sat there treading water for a moment getting my bearings, then I swam over to the shore. I sat there panting screaming back and forth with my friends:

"Feet went through my shoes!"

"Fuck!"

"Forgot to point my toes!"

"Hurt?!"

"No!"

"Bottom?!"

"No!"

Neither of them jumped. I started climbing up the rocky slope of the dam, my broken shoes making it difficult. Halfway up one of them jumped. I watched. I counted three long seconds before he hit. Then that moment when you aren't sure they will come back up. Then the surface water breaking. Then the yell of victory. This of course led my other friend to do the same.

When I got to the top I lit a cigarette and watched my friends clamber up the rocks. Both had remembered to point their toes. When they reached me they both lit cigarettes. There was a brief moment when we thought we might do it again, but then we thought we had made too much noise and should probably get the hell out of there before anybody showed up and busted us.

This was July. I was sixteen. And that was the nerve I would need if I was to get out of this rotten fucking shit hole of a town I was born in.

It was Saturday night, and I was late. The dashboard on my friend's BMW said it was eleven. My curfew was midnight. The dam was thirty miles from Thermopolis and another thirty to W. But the canyon was slow and steep. If we got stuck behind an RV I was screwed. My friend kept telling me to stop being a pussy, and my other friend in the back seat was telling me the same shit as he loaded the one-hitter.

I could hear him lighting up as J turned up the music. I was being droned out. Fucking dicks. I probably didn't need to worry, but Justin didn't have a curfew, and Clayton was eighteen, so it didn't matter to him either. But then, they didn't have to deal with my mom when they got home. And how do you explain to your mom that you were late because you and your friends were jumping off the dam? You don't. That's how.

When we got to Thermopolis we pulled into the Maverick for gas. Justin got out. He put five dollars in. At that time that meant nearly five gallons. When he was done he knocked on the window and made a circling motion with his hand that meant I should roll it down. The windows were electric. The car was turned off. I opened the door:

—You dicks got a dollar? —

I fumbled in my pocket. All I had was seventy cents. I gave it to him. Clayton reached over my head and handed him a dollar. I closed the door. We watched as Justin went inside. There were three locals standing by the entrance. He said something we couldn't hear. They all recoiled in a way that meant trouble. Clayton said, oh shit. We watched him pay and come out. There was a small altercation, but Justin managed to talk himself out of it. When he got back to the car he was smiling. He had a hard pack of cigarettes he was smacking against the palm of his hand. Packing them down.

— Fucking pussies. —

He opened the cigarettes and took one out. He lit it. He started the car. He turned around slowly in the gas station lot. As we got back onto the highway Justin burned rubber. All three of us turned our heads to watch the locals' faces become slack and then angry. They ran to their trucks and hopped in. Each one had their own truck. Haul ass! Clayton yelled from the back seat. They're coming!

Justin hit the gas. Luckily we hit the light just as it

turned yellow, otherwise they would have chased us out of town and probably followed us halfway to Worland before overtaking the car and beating the shit out of us.

As it was though, we were able to cruise easily up the main hill out of town, past the thermal pools and buffalo and head back down Highway 20.

The rest of the ride was mellow. Clayton kept trying to get me to smoke, but I wouldn't so he just blew it in my face from behind my ear, and Justin kept calling me a pussy every time he purposely ran over a rabbit and I complained. These were my friends. These were my only friends.

I was home by midnight thank god. As I got out of the car Clayton got into the front seat. I told my friends I would see them tomorrow, and Justin responded by flicking his cigarette at me and peeling out, most likely waking my dad up. Fucking dick. These were my friends. My only friends.

I walked around the block hoping the air would take the smell of cigarettes and weed off my clothes. The nighthawks were out eating bugs that flew under the street lamps. All the neighbors' lights were out. It was quite peaceful. I took my time.

When I got back home I smelled my fingers and went inside. My mom was still up. She was lying on the couch watching television. I said hi. She said:

"Hi honey, there's spaghetti in the fridge."

"Thanks, not hungry."

"You get up to tonight?"

"Dragging main."

I went into the bathroom. I washed my hands and

brushed my teeth. We only had one bathroom. The house was a ranch house. It had two bedrooms and a basement. Me and my two younger brothers shared one of the bedrooms upstairs. My parents had the other, and my older brother had the basement. My oldest brother was in college.

When I came out of the bathroom I told my mom goodnight and went to bed. Both my brothers were asleep. I took off my clothes and got into bed. I was thinking of the evening when another thought occurred to me. I was being as discrete as possible, but the motion of my bed was rocking my youngest brother's bed and he woke up. He asked me what I was doing. I told him I was rocking myself to sleep. He said that it felt nice and to keep doing it. I abandoned what I was doing and rocked him to sleep. Before long I was asleep myself.

In the morning it was Sunday. My dad was making pancakes and fried venison. I ate two plates. Around ten the phone rang. It was for me. Justin. He said he was coming over. I told him to meet me at the Mini Mart. I told my mom I was going out. She asked me where I was going. I told her to the hills. She said ok, be home by ten.

The church bells were ringing as I walked through the churches parking lot. They were so loud that anything pretty about them was dissipated, like getting slapped in the face by a tree branch. I crossed main and went into the Mini Mart. I bought a package of cigarettes. I went outside and waited. I packed the hard pack. I opened the package. I took one out. I looked at the end and made sure there was enough paper showing. I lit it.

Five minutes went by. I finished the cigarette. I grew bored. I walked over to the pay phone and dialed a number. It was a number of ceaseless entertainment. 1-800-HOT-BOYS. It was always the same message:

"You've reached one eight hundred Hot Boys, if you

would like to speak to a Hot Boy dial one nine hundred Hot Boys, for the most erotic Hot Sex on the phone."

It was a man's voice. He seemed like he really meant it. A few moments later Justin showed up in his BMW. I hung up the phone and got in.

On our way out of town we had to pick up Clayton. He lived behind the bentonite plant by the junkyard.

When we got to his house we parked the car and went inside. His mom was a hair dresser and Sunday was busy for her. She wasn't home. We went into the basement.

Clayton's room was in the basement. He was just waking up. He was listening to death metal and smoking from a bong. He handed the bong to Justin. He took a hit. He handed it to me. I took one too. Clayton went to take a shower. Me and Justin sat there waiting. I got stoned.

When Clayton was done with his shower he dressed and we went outside and got back into Justin's car. I was relegated to the back seat. This was fine with me. The front seat is too much responsibility. We got on the road leading east. Up past the Mormon church, and onto the highway.

When we got to Rattle Snake Ridge we pulled onto a dirt road. This was a grated dirt road. Bumpy but easy to navigate. About a mile in we turned right on a dirt road that was mainly struts. The going was slow. It took us nearly thirty minutes to go two miles.

When we stopped we were surrounded by hills. There was sagebrush on everything. Rabbits running around. Antelope barking at us. Derricks pumping for oil. Dry heat. The smell of silence.

We got out of the car. We all lit cigarettes. Justin opened the trunk. There was a small bag. In that bag were two pipe bombs. The bag was made of canvas. The bombs were made of lead.

We took the bag and walked up over one of the hills.
When we got to the other side we sat down. Justin asked
us if we were ready. Me and Clayton just smiled. Justin
stood up and lit the bomb and threw it. It exploded
wonderfully. All three of us ran over to check out the
damage. The damage was wonderful.

The next bomb, we decided, needed to be thrown
from the top of a hill for greater effect. We walked down.
Then we walked up. We were on top of the hill. Justin
lit the fuse and threw the bomb. Nothing happened. We
waited. Nothing happened.

We waited. Nothing happened. Then we talked:

"Fuck that, I ain't going down."

"The fuck I am."

"You threw the bitch."

"So what."

"Fucking pussy."

"Well at least go look."

"Like hell."

"Let's all go then."

"Fuck."

"Fuck that."

"Smoke first?"

We smoked a cigarette. Afterwards we moved slowly
to where he had thrown it. None of us wanted to find it.

In fact none of us did.

When we gave up looking we went back to the car.
We crept back slowly towards the main dirt road. We got
high-centered twice. Clayton and I had to get out and
push. When we got to the main road we loaded the one-
hitter and we decided to take the back roads into town.
By the time we made the highway it was nearly three.
And we were by Washakie Ten.

꧁꧂

Washakie Ten. Washakie County Road Number Ten. When I was younger I always thought it was called Washakie Ten because it was ten miles long. To this day I don't know if the road is that long or not. Seems about right. Ten miles at forty miles an hour, about seventeen minutes, that's ten miles right? Roughly?

We pulled off the highway and onto Washakie Ten. Clayton handed the one-hitter to the back, to me. We were immediately stuck behind a truck hauling sugar beets to the factory in town. I took a hit and handed it back. This was a terrible road during harvest. Either you got stuck behind trucks heading into town that were so weighed down that they could barely go twenty, or you tried to pass and couldn't because the trucks coming back to pick up more beets were in a hurry and were barreling down the road with underage drivers with work permits.

Every time we tried to pass, another huge empty dump truck with a thirteen-year old driver would appear. Half the time the trucks looked like nobody was driving because the kid was so short you couldn't see him from our perspective, being low to the ground, in a car. It was a little unnerving. The weed didn't help.

After the fourth attempt Justin was able to pass the truck in front of us. There was clear road for about a mile before we got stuck behind another truck. Justin gave up then. There was no rush. Clayton handed him the one-hitter. He used his elbows to drive as he lit the pipe. He handed it back to me. I finished it.

There was a brief moment of peace as we drove. Both windows were rolled down. The radio was off. Nobody said anything. On our left were fields of wheat and corn that led all the way to the base of Rattle Snake Ridge. On our right were fields of mostly sugar beets that led all the way to the highway into town, and on the side of the road a ditch. And in that ditch asparagus grew. And us driving at twenty miles an hour, with nothing to say to each other in the middle of summer, half-high on weed, and smelling good smells. It would almost make you relax. But we were teenagers. We couldn't relax.

Clayton couldn't take the silence. He opened the glove box and found a cassette tape. He shoved it into the tape deck. It was already loud. He made it louder. This made Justin grow impatient. He took the next right he could, even knowing it was private land, and hit the gas. We were going fifty before the grating bumps caused us to fishtail. It was pure luck we didn't end up in the ditch. He slowed down. As we drove by the farmer's house Clayton flipped the house the bird. I turned around to look out the window and make sure nobody was following us. Nobody was.

When we got to the highway we took a left. I was still looking back to see if anyone was following. Nobody was. It took us three minutes to get to the town's limits. The highway was faster.

Justin pulled into the A&W. Both he and Clayton worked there. We parked the car in the employee parking lot, which was just a little chunk of flat dirt across the alley, and we got out. Clayton lifted the latch that made the front seat move forward. This was a nice thing he would hardly ever do. I questioned his motives. When I got out I shut the door.

The day was Sunday. The parking lot was full. This A&W was still a drive-in. There were still menu boards. Teenagers would still come out to your car with calibers of change. The place was a novelty.

I followed my friends inside. There was a line to the

counter. The place had a salad bar. The chairs had green seating. The frames were white. My dad did that. Justin went to the bathroom. Clayton and I waited in line. When he came out, we were still waiting.

When we got to front of the line I ordered a burrito deluxe which has chili and onions and cheese. It comes in a Styrofoam hutch. It cost $1.19. Both Clayton and Justin ordered bacon burger deluxes. They got the discount.

Theirs came first of course, and they both grumbled for half the time it took for mine to come. They gave up complaining and went back to the car. I waited.

By the time I got my burrito they were waiting near the exit in the car. Justin was revving the engine, telling me to come on. Clayton was looking annoyed and smoking a cigarette. Fucking dicks.

I walked around the side of the car and tried to get in. The door was locked. Clayton was just laughing. I set my burrito on top of the car. I tried the door again. Just then Justin peeled out and my burrito fell on the ground. I didn't know what to do. I kicked the car. This made him get out and yell, what the fuck, why you kicking my car.

I stared at him. He stared backed. I kept staring, of course I wanted him to say he was sorry and I would say I was sorry and that would be that, but he didn't. He just got in the car. Slammed the door. Sped off.

I stood there looking at them drive away. Then the burrito. My dollar nineteen. Fucking dicks.

I looked over and could see people were watching me out the windows of the A&W, sitting on the seats my father had made. I was about to cry, but fuck that. Those days are over.

❧

I picked up my burrito. I scooped as much of its guts as I could back into its Styrofoam container. I threw it in the trash. I wanted to punch those jerks. I walked back through the parking lot. I took a right at the alley.

The alleys in W were all dirt. Hard dirt. Still are. Hard dirt and gravel. I walked by the motel and the snow mobile shop. I crossed Yellowstone and stayed in the alley. There was nothing but wooden fences and dumpsters for the next block. Piles of mown grass. Trailers. Dogs barking and silence. The next block was the same. The block after that was slightly different. As I was crossing the street I could hear a hush shish sound. I was still feeling sorry for myself and didn't notice the noise until I got close to the dumpster it was coming from. I still didn't notice until the dumpster lid rose up a foot and said my name. I said:

"Jesus Donny what the fuck you in the dumpster for?"

"Oh man, oh man, no look, can't you see what I am wearing?"

He lifted the lid up. He was dressed in an orange jumpsuit. I just then noticed the hand cuffs.

"You see any cops? Man dude! Fucking hell!"

He dropped back down into the dumpster. I didn't know what to do, so I just kept walking. I crossed the parking lot of the clinic that was across the street from the police station and the jail. I watched three police men run out and get into their cars and speed off. I smiled and took a left on Robertson.

When I got back home my older brother was throwing a baseball at the side of the house. He had drawn a square on the chimney. The chimney was cosmetic. There was no fire place. I watched him for a while. He was good. It was nice to see him in action. Every time he threw the ball it cracked against the bricks, but then it hit the grass and didn't roll back to him. He had to go fetch it. He needed a catcher. He didn't have one.

I went inside to grab my mitt. My mom was in the living room ironing. She ironed clothes for extra money. She said:

"You're home early."

"Yeah."

I grabbed my mitt from me and my brothers' room and ran back outside.

My brother was a wild pitcher. He had speed but he lacked focus. He holds the state record for pole vault for this reason. Run as fast as you can toward this hole and shove a pole inside. See what transpires. Have the courage to hold on. When you get to the top let go. And then the grace of birds. But not with his fastball.

I sat spread legged in front of the fake chimney and told him about Donny in the dumpster. He was winding up, but then he stopped:

"Really?"

"Yeah, he was wearing handcuffs."

"What, he broke out of jail?"

"I don't know, I guess."

"Guess that was those sirens."

"Guess so."

"Shit."

He threw the ball. I caught it barely, by standing up.

My older brother threw balls at me until sundown. Half of them hit the side of the house. It was lucky we didn't break any windows. When the nighthawks came out our mother came out. She told us dinner was ready if we wanted it. We went inside.

Dinner was spaghetti and meat sauce. Both our younger brothers were eating when we got inside. Our dad too. And our mom. We went into the kitchen and got some food. I ate mine sitting on the floor and woke up an hour later with my brothers and my mom laughing at me. My older brother had gone out, and my dad had gone to bed. I put my plate on the table nearest to me. I went to bed.

In the morning my dad woke me up. He did so by tickling the bottom of my foot. It was five. Mondays were trash days. It was still dark outside. It took me a minute to get out of bed.

When I finally got out of bed I put my pants on. I put on a t-shirt that said Kenny's Lawn Care. The shirt was green. I went into the living room and shut the bedroom door. My father had left it open to remind me to wake up. My brothers could keep sleeping. I went into the bathroom and took a piss. When I came out my father handed me a cup of coffee. We sat there in silence. He was lacing his boots. He always wore Lines Men's boots which I never understood, because whenever I wore them they were too heavy, and in the winter they made your feet cold for no reason. I never asked him why. This was a perfect time to ask him, but I didn't. I instead asked him what he was doing today. He told me:

"Roof out by Renner's. There's pancakes if you're hungry."

"Thanks, maybe."

"Got enough sunblock? Supposed to be hot."

"Think so."

"Ok."

He went into the kitchen and filled his thermos with coffee. He said ok again and left. I could hear his truck idle when he opened the front door to the house. It was a diesel. He had started it when I was in the bathroom. He closed the door.

I sat there alone, drinking my coffee. I wasn't hungry so I didn't eat any pancakes. I did put on sunscreen. I finished my coffee and brushed my teeth. I went outside and sat on the porch. I lit a cigarette and waited.

When the truck showed up Skip was hanging half outside of the window smoking a cigarette. He smiled and waved at me. The driver was the owner of the company. He was looking straight ahead. They were pulling a trailer that had three-foot high metal walls. The walls were painted black and said: Kenny's Lawn Care. I jumped in the trailer.

The runners were wood and the trailer was bumpy. There was no weighing it down but myself. I didn't mind. When we stopped next we picked up Hank, who was the same age as me. He hopped in the trailer and said hi.

As we headed out of town he bummed a cigarette. It took him three tries to light it. It was too windy to talk. The sun was starting to rise.

Monday was trash day. Which meant, on Mondays, we collected trash from the houses that were outside the city limits, but were too close to town to burn it. This meant we went door to door dumping fifty gallon metal barrels into the back of the trailer and taking the trash to the dump. It was gross and took much longer than it needed to. It was always a long day, and always ended unhappily at the dump, which was a dusty, smelly place out by the Telephone road.

Hank and I always wore gloves. There was something

about what we were doing though, that, being teenagers, was titillating. Maybe we could find some nudie mags!

We never did. It was always just smelly Styrofoam and dead cats. We had to pile the cats to the side because they went into the animal pit. Sometimes there were raccoons.

Part of me was glad about this because on some Sundays I was the guy that let people into the dump.

On Mondays we just dealt with the out-of-town trash. Tuesdays and Wednesdays were days we mowed. Thursdays were the rich clients. And Fridays and Saturdays were off. But Sundays…

So on Thursday Kenny dropped me off at the Decker house to do a trim of the whole yard. Which meant clearing the driveway of debris and cutting tree branches, but on this day I kept hearing a noise. It sounded like a child screaming. I quit cutting branches to investigate. The noise was in the backyard. Behind the house. I was nervous at first because it did in fact sound like a child. The part of me that was curious was scared. The part of me that was scared was curious. I found the noise. It was a goat that had put its head through the fence. His horns had stuck him. He couldn't get back. I spent half the afternoon trying to help him understand that he could just put his head back on his neck and pull back. He didn't understand. When I finally realized this I grabbed his horns and tried to push him back through the fence. He resisted. He kept resisting. In the end I yanked his head through the fence, which startled him, and in his moment of flaccid panic I shoved his head back through the fence.

I only mention this because on the next Sunday, Kenny had me running the dump. Clayton and Justin were still mad at me about the whole A&W incident, and I hadn't heard from them the whole week. Fuck those assholes. So on Sunday my dad woke me early, and I borrowed my brother's car to mind the entrance to the dump.

My oldest brother's car was a B210 Datsun. The solenoid was out, so you had to start it by arcing the battery, which meant you turned the key to the start position, opened the hood and stabbed a screwdriver into the battery that you connected with the solenoid. It made a thump sound. Then the engine started.

On this Sunday, I drove my brother's car to the dump. Over the Big Horn River, past the Graveyard and the Fair Grounds, past the Highway Department, and the Firemen Training Depot with its three story tall concrete building that they make the volunteers carry heavy bags of sand up to the top as training, and instead of taking a left on Fifteen Mile, I take a right on the Dump Road, the place where antelope are always standing stupid and confused waiting to be run over.

The Datsun can barely do forty, so the antelope are safe. Not only that, but the Datsun is a tin can. It would crumple if it hit anything more than fifty pounds.

I got to the dump gates. I had the keys. I opened the gates. I drove down the road that leads me to the little hut that is where I am supposed to wait for people to come in. I parked my brother's car. I sat in the hut. I had a book. I tried to read it.

Two hours went by. Nobody came. I got bored. I spent a long time looking at the fence that surrounds the dump. There was a lot of trash blowing around. I thought about going out and grabbing the trash. This is when someone came, all of the sudden, and there was so much dust I closed the door of the hutch and waited. He had a refrigerator and two dead sheep. I told him where to go. When he left I went to go look at the animal pit. The dead sheep were lying on a dead cow. Him throwing the sheep on the cow made its guts explode. It was too gross. I ran away.

Another hour went by. I got bored again. I had a thought. There was a huge tire in the tire pit. I thought it might be cool to roll it down the hill that made up the pit proper.

Nobody came. I decided yes. I went down and started to drag the huge tire up the hill.

The tire was heavy. I couldn't roll it. It would just roll back on me. I had to drag it. This was nice.

An hour later a truck showed up and I had to run down and tell him where to go. Right after I ran back up and drug the tire further. Another hour passed. Then another truck. Then another pull on the tire. Then nothing. I was at the top of the hill.

I stood there waiting for somebody to come. Nobody did. I could see most of the town in front of me. A bunch of stupid antelope. Barking like idiots. And the dump fence, pointless and weak. I let the tire roll. It was glorious. It barreled through the trash and through the fence. It ended up somewhere down and out of the way. I laughed and went back to the hutch.

The next day was Monday again. It started the same way the previous Monday had. My father tickling the bottom of my foot at five A.M. This time he wasn't around when I finally managed to get out of bed. He must have been working in Cody or something, a two-hour drive. I poured a cup of coffee and looked at the pancakes he had made. Five is just too early to eat. Even if you are a teenager. I brushed my teeth and took my coffee to the porch. I sat down on the steps and lit a cigarette. The newspaper boy came, he was a man in his forties. He handed the paper to me without a word. I put the paper down next to my coffee.

The morning was chilly, but you could tell it was going to get hot. The automatic sprinklers from the neighbor's yard across the street came on. It was five twenty. I knew this because I was there when Kenny had set the timer after we installed the sprinklers. He had told me:

"There ain't no point in running these things after the sun comes up, just wasting water." I nodded. He said this every time he set one of these timers, either to me or some other teenager he was paying seven dollars an hour to help him.

I finished my coffee and stood up. I threw my cigarette butt towards the street and bent down and picked up the paper. I went inside and put the paper on the living room table. I put my coffee cup in the sink. I went back out onto the porch and waited.

Five minutes went by before Kenny pulled the truck and trailer in front of our house. Skip was once again hanging out the passenger side window smoking a cigarette. I ran and jumped into the trailer.

The day was quite uneventful. I got a sunburn and everything smelled bad. It's hard to understand how bad trash can smell. Especially a week's worth of trash in a fifty-gallon metal barrel that has been stewing in the summer desert heat of north-central Wyoming. It's pretty smelly. And it just gets smellier. Used to be you could just burn it, but they kept changing the city limits, so now you would need to be halfway to Thermopolis before you could burn your trash, but by then you were in Thermopolis' city limits and they wouldn't let you burn it either.

By the time I got home I was dirty and gross. It was just after four and nobody was home. I ran a bath. Our mother had decided showers were too messy and had grown tired of cleaning up after us, although I don't ever remember the bathtub having a shower curtain, or her ever cleaning the bathroom. As the water filled the tub I laid down on the floor and masturbated. Like always I had pushed my foot against the door as I did so. The bathroom had a lock, but it was not trustworthy, and god knows who was about to come barreling in.

When I finished I cleaned myself up and got in the bath. It was slightly cool. I soaked for a while before standing up and using the bar of soap to scrub the eleven hours of grime I had acquired. I sat back down and rinsed off. I used my foot to pull the drain lever down. I stood up and got out. I dried off. I turned the faucet back on and scrubbed the ring off the walls of the bathtub. I wrapped the towel around my waist and gathered my dirty clothes. I took the dirty clothes to the washing machine that was in the pantry. I took my belt from my jeans. I removed the things from my pockets. I put clothes in the washer. I went into me and my brothers' room. I found some clean boxers and put them on. I rooted around in a great big bucket of socks and found a similar pair. I found a clean pair of jeans, size thirty-six by thirty-six. The same size we all wore, the same size that fit my dad. I put them on and went back into the pantry to get my belt and things. I had to hold them up as I walked. The pants were way too big for me. As I was putting the belt on the phone rang. I went into the living room. I answered it. It was Justin, the jerk that ruined my burrito. After I said hello he said:

"What's up dick bone, still acting like a cock knock?" This was his version of an apology.

"I don't know." I never knew what to say when he insulted me, I needed his approval for some reason.

"You doin? Done with work?"

"Talkin to you ain't I?" This was my version of forgiveness.

"I'm coming by, Clayton's mom's at work."

"Now?"

"Leaving."

"Ok, I'll write…" He had hung up, "A note" was how I was going to end that sentence. I hung up the phone.

I wrote a note to my mom that said:

Going out with Justin and Clay. Will be home by eleven.

I went outside and sat on the porch. I lit a cigarette. It was still hot so I went around the corner of the house to stand in the shade.

As I was waiting my dad came home and caught me smoking. He told me not to let my mom catch me doing that. He went inside. Justin showed up and I got in his car. I slammed the door and he yelled at me. His passenger side door either slammed or didn't shut at all. It was annoying he always yelled at you for it. I said sorry.

As we drove out of town towards Clayton's we listened to music. It was too loud to talk. I was still a little pissed about the burrito incident from the week before, but I kept it to myself. I don't think he ever gave it a second thought. Both our windows were rolled down and it smelled like dust and ditches as we reached the highway. By the time it smelled like corn we were driving so fast we had to roll the windows up. When we got to the bentonite plant we slowed down and took a left. We passed the junkyard and crossed the weighing station. There were loaders making dust. We left the windows rolled up. When we got to Clayton's house a dog came out to meet us. I got out and petted him. He followed us inside.

༄༅༄

Clayton's mom was a hairdresser. She was rarely home. I don't think this was the reason why she was rarely home. She was just rarely home.

Justin and I and the dog let ourselves in. We used the side door that went straight to the basement. To the stairs that went straight to the basement. Down to the basement.

When we got to Clayton's room he was sitting on his bed smoking a bong. He was listening to music. The music was aggressive. He blew smoke out and said:

"Why you bring the dog?"

"He followed us," I said.

"Fuck that, out!" He yelled at the dog, "Tony get!" The dog's name was Tony.

I sat down on the floor. Justin kept standing. Clayton handed me the bong. I took a rip and handed it to Justin. He took a rip. He handed it back to Clayton and sat down in a beanbag chair in the corner. For the next thirty minutes nobody said anything. We just listened to music and took bong rips. Eventually the dog came back down. Clayton yelled:

"Tony roll out! I already told you to roll!"

Tony laid down next to me. I petted him. He was a nice dog. This irritated Clayton but he didn't do anything. He loved Tony. Another thirty minutes went by. Justin got up from the beanbag and said:

"Let's do something."

We all stood up. Tony too. We went back outside. Clayton told Tony to stay as we got into the car. I got in the back seat. As we drove back towards the highway Justin asked me for a smoke. As he reached around to get it he almost drove us into a giant propane tank. Clayton said Jesus Christ! I laughed.

Once we were on the highway we had nowhere to go. We took a right and headed into town. Hold on! Clayton said, turn around. Fuck that, why? I forgot, I got a six pack. We pulled over to the side of the road. We waited for a truck to pass. We turned around.

When we got back to his house he got out and went inside. When he came back out he had a six-pack of beer and a pistol. He got back in the car. Tony was following him. He yelled out the window to tell him to stay. Justin said:

"Fifteen Mile?"

"Why not."

"You ain't too stoned?"

"Nope."

We had to go through town. Past the water tower with the graffiti that read, "Eat Butts" and the movie house that was playing movies that were released two months ago. We had to cross the river and take a left at the cemetery. Right next to the fairgrounds. Before long we were on a dirt road. That dirt road was called Fifteen Mile because it was fifteen miles long.

About three miles in we pulled off the main dirt road to the left and on to a path that was mainly ruts and cottonwood trees. He stopped by a culvert, where the canal crosses the creek. The creek was dry this time of the year. We got out of the car. Clayton handed us each a beer. I drank all of mine in a single drink without thinking about it. He told me to put it over there. The empty can. Over there was by the canal, and it smelled like reeds and wet dirt.

When I got back to the car he was holding the pistol. He aimed it at the can. I plugged my ears. He shot twice and nothing happened but noise. Justin came around the car and said:

"Fucking give me that!" He grabbed it from his hands. Clayton smiled. He knew Justin was a worse shot than he was. He fired the remaining four shots. The pistol was a

.45 revolver. I plugged my ears the whole time. He never hit the can.

"Fuck it!" he yelled, "I'm going for a walk!" He shoved the gun into Clayton's hands. He stormed off. We laughed. I laid down on the dirt and looked up at the sky. Clayton put the gun in the car through the open window and lit a cigarette. He sat down next to me. He said:

"I'm sick of this shit shop."

"What, Justin?"

"No, he's ok, he's just a retard, this town."

"But what?"

"I don't know."

Funny thing about this conversation, as stupid as it was, it would change my entire life.

When Justin got back from his walk he didn't want to hang out anymore. He got into the car and started it. Clayton and I got in. When we got to 15th he pulled the car over. I got out. Clayton slammed the door. I could hear Justin yelling at him about slamming the door as they drove away. He would save himself a lot of grief if he would just fix that door.

I waited for the light and crossed the street. I passed the courthouse. There is a statue of Chief Washakie on the lawn of the courthouse. I stopped and looked at it like always. The statue is comical, it's just his head, but with a huge feather headdress, it's comical because the statue is like fifteen feet tall and out of proportion, his nose is huge and beaklike, his eyes are beady and he has an elongated neck. The statue itself is too skinny for its size. I guess it was meant as a tribute, but it seems like it's just mocking history. It's hard to wrap your head around.

I guess this is why I stopped to look at it, but I doubt it, I think I just stop because it's weird and out of place.

I stopped looking and went on walking. I passed the bank and the Crossbow. The bank's flashing sign said it was 8:17 P.M. and that it was 89 degrees Fahrenheit. The sun was setting. The Crossbow's parking lot was full. Inside all the booths looked full. The place seemed busy. I crossed the street and went to the Mini Mart. I still had another three hours before I had to be home. I didn't know what to do. I went to the payphone and dialed 1-800-HOT-BOYS. I listened to the recording a couple times and laughed. I hung up. I stood there for a minute wondering what to do. I took out my pack of cigarettes and was about to light one when I realized I was standing next to a stack of propane tanks. I went around the corner. I lit the cigarette.

The Mini Mart was next to the pizza place where Skip, the guy that was always hanging out the window smoking when Kenny picked me up on Monday mornings, delivered pizza in on the evenings. He happened to come out the back door carrying pizzas. Going on a delivery. I called his name. He saluted me for some reason and got in his car and went on his delivery. He was a weird dude. I liked him enough, but I didn't know what he was up to. He had been waiting for his mom to die for quite some time, apparently she had money and a house that he would inherit. I think he was in his forties, but I don't know, I was sixteen, so he could have been anywhere between twenty-five and sixty-two for all I knew, all adults were ancient. But he was waiting for his mom to die, for the big payout, and all he had to do was wait her out. He worked two jobs, the one with me, and the one with the pizza. I really don't know why, he lived with his mom, I can't imagine she made him pay much rent, and he had a girlfriend. I think the girlfriend had ideas.

I finished my cigarette just as a car came down the alley. It was dark enough now that the car had its headlights on. It turned into the parking lot blinding me. I moved out of the way. I was standing next to the air compressor. You don't approach the Mini Mart that way unless you want to use the air compressor. From the alley, I mean. I was wrong and I should have known it. Known it the second I smelt chewing tobacco.

"Hey faggot, waiting for somebody to blow you off?" He wasn't being clever. I didn't say anything. "I'm talking to you fuck stain!" I stood there staring until my eyes adjusted. I knew who it was of course, I knew it before I smelled the tobacco, but I was still thinking about Skip and his conniving girlfriend.

When my eyes finally adjusted I could see there was four dudes in the car. Part of me said fuck, but the other part of me, the teenager part said:

"Fuck you!" I flipped him off and ran.

Luckily there were two trucks gassing up as I ran towards Main. Jeff and his three goons would have to back up and go around the corner. I ran across the street almost causing a crash, well, not a crash, a twenty-mile an hour fender bender, and ran through the parking lot of the parts store and took a left at the alley. I ran two blocks down the alley and hid behind a dumpster. It smelled like cut grass and dog shit. I waited.

To this day I am still surprised how prescient these assholes were. Maybe they could smell the fear? Maybe they were treating me like a rabbit and knew I would hide instead of run? It doesn't matter really, but they pulled right in front of the dumpster I was hiding behind and stopped.

They got out. Jeff left the car running. It was from the seventies so the engine rocked the body, even as it idled. I was trapped. He said:

"You little fucking punk, get out here!"

"Yeah, you fucking punk!"

"Punk faggot!"

"Faggot!"

It was a derivative of language. They were *Killing The MAth*. Reducing thought into violence.

I stayed as silent as I could. Not breathing. Waiting.

The four of them poked around for a while. Luckily they had a leader which meant they didn't think for themselves, otherwise they would have acted like animals and found me, and probably tore me to shreds, but that didn't happen.

Eventually he said:

"Fuck it! The little fucking bitch ain't here."

"Little shit."

"Fucking bitch."

"Bitch."

They got back in the car and drove off. I waited for a while, listening. The moon came out. The evening was cooling down. I was only wearing a t-shirt. I started getting cold. Fuck it. They probably already gave up looking for me. I came out from my hiding place behind the cut grass and dog shit. I lit a cigarette. I walked home.

It's funny how quiet shit can get. That the absence of sound can create distance. That the ears crave company, searching, in desperate need of a companion. I imagine that thoughts are just the result of the ears screaming at the brain to:

'just say something, anything, just tell me you are with me, here, now!'

It was this kind of silence that surrounded me as I

walked home. The gravel under my feet, visceral. A dog barking three blocks over and two houses down, behind a chain linked fence. The sound of a television. A train passing through town, slowly. The ding of the rail arms dropping, stopping traffic. Somebody, a man yelling, 'No it's diesel!' followed by a door slamming. The gas station.

This was all useless noise to me. To my ears. To my brain. I was listening instead for the sound of the car that would come and spit four horrible jerks out of its doors that would beat me into a pulp. They never came. I got home safely.

When I got inside I walked into the living room. My two younger brothers were playing a video game and my mom was lying on the couch reading a magazine. She said:

"Hi honey, you're home early."

"Yeah."

"There's spaghetti in the fridge."

I went into the kitchen and opened the refrigerator. There was two huge plastic bags filled with spaghetti noodles. I took one out. I put it on the counter. I went back into the fridge and took the pot out that contained the sauce. I put it on the counter. I took a plate from the cupboard and put it on the counter. I reached into the bag of noodles and pulled out a handful. I put it on the plate. I took the lid off the sauce and put it on top of the bag of noodles. I looked around to find a large spoon to scoop the sauce out. My mom yelled:

"Cover it!"

"Ok!" I yelled back.

I scooped a bunch of sauce on the spaghetti. I covered it with plastic wrap. I put it in the microwave. I pushed the button for two minutes. I poured myself a glass of milk. My mom yelled:

"There's bread in the cabinet!"

"Ok!"

I didn't want any bread. I put a fork in my pocket and waited for the spaghetti. When it was done cooking I took it out of the microwave and took the plastic wrap off. I threw the plastic wrap in the trash and took the plate of spaghetti and my glass of milk into the living room. I sat down on the couch. The other couch. The one my mom wasn't reading her magazine on. I put my things on the table in front of it. I took the fork from my pocket. I started eating. I watched my brothers' video game. My mom said:

"What'cha been doing honey?"

"Stuff, I suppose."

"Stupid stuff is my guess," my second youngest brother said.

"Oh, shut up," my mom said.

"Yeah, shut up, dingle berry, oh shit, you missed it!" I was watching the game, "Go left!"

"I can't they're gonna…"

I watched my brothers play video games until they had to go to bed. I ate another plate of spaghetti, this time with bread. The bread with butter. I drank another glass of milk. I fell asleep on the couch while my mom watched reruns. I woke up when my older brother came home. My mom said:

"Hi honey, there's spaghetti in the fridge."

"It's still out," I said.

"I'm ok." he went straight downstairs and to his room. Music started playing as soon as he got there. I was hoping he would eat something so I didn't have to clean up. But he didn't. So I cleaned up.

When I was finished putting the spaghetti away I went into the bathroom and peed. I brushed my teeth. I told my mom goodnight. I went to bed.

❦

The next morning my mom woke me up. She did it by opening the door and saying:

"Honey, it's seven."

I heard her go into the bathroom and shut and lock the door. Then I heard the bathwater running. She had been up since six I am certain. The sun was out already. I had no problem getting out of bed. I could still hear the bathwater running as I walked into the living room. I had to piss so I went through the kitchen and out the back door. Had it been dark still I would have just pissed off the back porch. Instead I walked down the wooden steps barefoot and onto the cold concrete sidewalk that led to the alley.

The corn in the garden was taller than me now, and took up most of the garden on the left of the sidewalk. There were stacks of flagstone to the right. My dad had plans to build a patio. I walked past the garage which made me gag a little.

My dad did taxidermy as well as carpentry. The garage was his shop and studio. He did European mounts, which meant rather than make the animal head look realistic he carved the hide and the flesh off the heads, put them in modified chest freezers that had special bugs that would eat the rest of the flesh off. Then he would boil the heads. Then bleach the heads in hydrogen peroxide. Sometimes a bug would get loose and make it to the house. If you found it you didn't kill it, you scooped it up and took it into the garage and put it in one of the coolers. If he was around you told him, then he would do it. The bugs were kind of scary, but also precious, he had paid a lot of money for them. He wanted to keep them alive.

The garage smelled like death. I walked by it. I gagged a little. I took a leak behind the dumpster. Behind the garage. I went back inside. There was coffee made. I poured myself a cup. I was hungry. I had time for breakfast.

I made myself spaghetti the same way I did the night before. I was eating it and drinking coffee while watching the television when my mom came out of the bathroom. She had a towel wrapped around her hair, around her head. She had a towel wrapped around her body as well. She held her nightclothes in her arms. She said:

"Morning honey, sleep ok?" She was doing something with her ear and a cotton swab.

"Slept fine. See this?" I motioned to the television.

"Hold on," she went back into the bathroom and ditched the cotton swab. She came back. "What is it? Wow, all week huh. Where you working?"

"I'm in town all week."

"Wear sunscreen, hold on I got some seventy, don't leave."

"Ok."

I finished my spaghetti and coffee. I went and made the same thing twice. I was not looking forward to working outside in hundred-plus weather all week. A thought did occur to me though, that maybe it would be too hot to work and I could go camping early this weekend. I was finishing my second spaghetti when my mom came back into the living room wearing a pantsuit. She had a job at the local phone company. She was an assistant to the regional manager. Her hair was still covered in a towel. She started putting on makeup in the mirror above the couch she liked to sit on. I said:

"Dad at Renner's all week?"

"No, just today, Dean's cabin is ready again, he's heading up there tomorrow."

"That's good, Cody should be cool enough."

"Shit, the sunscreen."

My mom hurried off into her room. I stood up and took my plate into the kitchen drinking the last of my coffee as I walked. I put my dishes in the sink. I put the spaghetti stuff away. When I got back into the living room she said:

"It's there on the table, honey."

"Thanks." She was again putting on makeup, but now her hair hung wet.

I took off my shirt and put sunscreen on every inch of my body above the top of my jeans. I didn't like sunburns. In weather like this they became brutal. I said:

"Thinking of going camping this weekend."

"With who?"

"Justin and Clay."

"Where?"

"Leigh Creek I guess, if it get's too hot, maybe go early?"

"Ok, you get your back?"

"Think I got it."

"Let me see," I turned around, "give me that!"

My mom made sure I had enough sunscreen on. I put on my shirt. I filled up a gallon of water. I brushed my teeth and went out front to wait on the porch. My mom was blowdrying her hair. I hated this sound.

It was hot already. I wanted to smoke, but I didn't dare do so in front of my mom. I just sat there in the shade waiting. When Kenny showed up Skip wasn't hanging out the window smoking like normal. The window was rolled up. The air conditioner was most likely on. He didn't have a trailer today, so I hopped in the back of the truck. There was three other boys in the back of the truck. I knew them all. I knew none of them well. I said hi and wished all the sudden I would have put ice in the gallon of water I had brought. I guessed by ten it would be too hot to drink.

I lit a cigarette as the truck pulled away from the curb. The other boys looked at me like I had just pulled a fire alarm. Like I was about to get in trouble. I ignored them until they stopped looking at me. There wasn't an actual thought that went through my head, but I knew this would be my last week working this job. I just couldn't process the point.

We were working on top of the hill. By the old water tower. The rich part of town. All the driveways were curved with an entrance and an exit. The houses themselves were two storied mansions with a separate two-car garage and bungalow. There was grass everywhere. Cottonwood trees. Not a Russian olive in sight. The truck pulled over. We all hopped out of the bed. Kenny and Skip got out of the cab leaving the engine running. Kenny pointed to three pallets of fertilizer stacked in white plastic bags. Four feet high. He said:

"This is it. Follow me." We followed him to the back of the house. There was nothing but dirt from the edge of the house to the start of the hill that dropped back into town. Also, from property line to property line. A mile's worth of dirt. He said:

"Use those two spreaders, me and Skip are going back to town to get some tools, the sod will be here at noon."

When they left it was decided that two of the boys would run the spreaders and me and the other boy would refill them as they went. We would start at the property line and meet in the middle.

The first bag was easy. Fifty pounds of granule thrown over the shoulder with a nice cool morning breeze. We lugged it to the back of the house and took our pocket knifes out. We cut a slit. We filled the spreaders. The second bag wasn't so bad except we had to meet the guys on the other end of the dirt, which had been tilled, which made it spongy. The third bag was easier, by distance, because they were back to the starting point, just two feet closer to the middle, but harder by weight because it was the third one in. Thirty minutes had gone by. It was five degrees hotter. The sun was on us now.

When the first pallet was finished we took a break. My water was already warm so I tried to drink as much as possible. I put the jug in some shade when I was finished. We all took off ours shirts. We broke into the second pallet.

By the end of the second pallet we were sweating. The plastic was sticking to our shoulders. Everyone had their sunglasses on except me. We took a break. The sun had moved in a way that I didn't notice was cooking my water. It was already too hot to drink. I drank it anyway. I found a place where spiders hang out and stuck it there, knowing it would be cooler. We broke the third pallet.

At this point it was just hot and sticky and miserable. We needed more sunscreen but we had left it in the truck. In the beginning of the day there was nice thoughts and music going through my head, now it was just weird birds. The sweat dripping from my face got into my eyes. The sunscreen made it sting. My belt dug into my hips. The heat made me nauseous. By the time we finished the third pallet it was eleven thirty. We found a patch of shade and waited. My water was gross but I could drink it. There were no spiders on it. It was too hot to smoke.

Kenny showed back up and backed his truck onto the driveway. He got out and took the tailgate down. He slid a ribbed orange three-gallon thermos with a white lid and white spigot to the edge. He put some cups next to it. He slid a cooler out. He opened the lid. Skip wasn't with him anymore. All four of us boys went and found our sunscreen. It was hot to the touch. It felt like my skin was sucking it in when I put mine on. We stood in line to get a glass of water. Kenny said:

"There's sandwiches and chips in the cooler, you get it done?" One of the boys said, "Yeah it's done."

We sat in the shade eating chips and ham and cheese sandwiches. Drinking ice-cold water. When we were finished, like clockwork, a truck pulled up with a trailer stacked with sod. Then another. Just looking at it made you feel dirty. Literally dirty. Kenny said to me:

"Let's lay the hose."

There were four thirty-foot hoses in the back of the truck. I grabbed one and took it to the backyard. It was hot. I wished I had gloves. I attached it to the spigot at the back of the house and stretched it to its limit. I did this three more times, connecting hose to hose. Finally I added a spray nozzle and turned the spigot on. I watched the hose turn rigid making sure there weren't any kinks. I went back to the front of the house.

I told Kenny it was done and he said:

"K boys, I'll get to hosing, start bringin em back."

There is nothing like a nice hunk of floppy sod being thrown over your sunburned shoulder in hundred-degree heat at dead noon in the rich part of town. It's like a slap to your face, but for your soul. The first ten or so were the worst because the dirt had dried, and the sod rolls had been cooking, but it got better. They cooled down the deeper you got, but it got worse because Kenny was hosing down the ground and all the sudden you were walking through mud, and you could watch your progress, so slow, so very slow, so hot and dirty and mud sticking to your shoes, and the sun, relentless.

By the time we were finished there was no need for sunscreen anymore. We were covered in dirt. We had stopped taking breaks because we wanted to be done. We just took a drink of water every time we got back to the truck. I had ditched my smokes and wallet because my pants were so sweaty, and one of the other boys had puked when he drank too much water. It was four in the afternoon when we got back into the bed of the truck. Nobody was clean enough to ride in the cab except Kenny, who was driving.

Nobody said anything as we rode back down the hill into town. The wind was nice. The slight cool from the canal that ran through town was nice too. I was the last one to be dropped off. Nobody said goodbye when I got out.

When I got to my front door I took off all my clothes and draped them over steps to dry. Nobody else was home. I went straight to bathroom and started the bath. I locked the door and masturbated. Standing up so I wouldn't get dirt everywhere. I cleaned up and got in the bath. My skin hurt from the sunburn. I washed my hair. There was a ring of filth when I drained the tub. I rinsed it down the drain. I unlocked the door and opened it. I yelled out to see if anyone was home. Nobody answered. I took my dirty underwear and walked into me and my brothers bedroom. I threw underwear on the floor and put a new pair on. I found a clean pair of pants and put them on. I put on a t-shirt and picked up my dirty underwear and took them to the dirty clothes bin by the washer and dryer. I went back to the front porch.

My smokes were in my pants. I took one out and lit it. I took my wallet out. I put it in my pocket. I sat on the porch, my white feet in the sun, pruned from being in the mud all day, the rest of my body in the shade, smoking. Just then my dad showed up. I didn't expect that, he said:

"Got some sun, huh? Don't let your mom catch you doing that." I stood up and went around the corner.

❧

As I stood there smoking next to the hedges that ran along the side of the house I could hear our neighbor watching television. She was coughing. She smoked constantly. She watched television and smoked. Sometimes she made cookies. She would bring them over. Nobody would eat them though because they tasted like cigarettes. I heard my dad go out the back door. The phone rang. I ran inside and answered it. I said:

"Hello."

"What's up pud-whack? Done working?" It was Justin, the one with the BMW .

"Yeah, I'm done."

"Come over, let's go to the pits."

"Why don't you just pick me up?"

"I'm eating a sandwich."

"Ok, let me get some shoes on."

I was putting some socks on when my dad came back in. He already smelled like death, he had been in the garage maybe two minutes. He said:

"You should put some more sun block on, that looks bad, going out?"

"Ok, I will, yeah."

"Leave a note for your mom." He went back outside.

I left a note for my mom telling her I was going to the pits and would be back by ten. I went out to the porch and put my muddy shoes back on. I started walking across town.

I took the alleys hoping to avoid Main. Main wasn't actually Main Street, it was Bighorn Avenue, but it wasn't that either, it was Highway 20, it was just called Main because it was the main street that ran through town, why it was called Bighorn is beyond me. Propriety? Can't imagine it matters, but it was best to be avoided. It was the social center of town. If you wanted your business known, that is where you went. Cops cruised Main. Your parents' friends cruised Main. Jerks that wanted to beat you up cruised Main. On Friday and Saturday night even you cruised Main, looking for beer and girls and fights. It was best to be avoided.

When I got to 13th I took a left and had no choice but to cross Main. I did so without incident and took a right at the alley behind the auto parts store. I heard a car approaching and tensed, the car was going slower than somebody that didn't know me. I stopped and turned around. I relaxed. It was only Donny the guy from the dumpster with handcuffs. He pulled over and put his car in park. He rolled his window down. He said:

"Got a smoke?" I took the cigarettes from my pocket and knocked two out. I handed him one. I put the other in my mouth.

"Soft pack, nice."

"I thought you were in jail?" There were three girls in the car with him, maybe thirteen years old. He lit the cigarette. I lit mine too.

"Nah, they were just about to release me."

"But why were you hiding in the dumpster?"

"Fuck them bitches, man."

"What'cha doin?"

"Cruisin, check it out," Donny had a plastic cup from Mini Mart resting between his legs, he held it up to me and took off the lid, he said, "Look, it's fucking brilliant, all ya gotta do is buy a drink and fucking dump that shit out, then you fill up a bag with whatever you want and put the straw in, and fuck, you can cruise Main and the cops don't know your huffin. Brilliant right?"

"Right."

"Yo, dog, gotta roll, you been alright?" He said this as he was rolling up his window and driving away. I didn't have time to answer. I guess he just stopped to brag.

When I got to Justin's I went to the back of his house

and knocked on the glass sliding doors. He didn't answer so I let myself in and went into the basement. He was lying on his bed listening to a record wearing headphones. His eyes were closed. I slapped the side of his foot. He had his shoes on. He opened his eyes and sat up. He unplugged the headphones. The music came barreling out like a fire eating a body on the Ganges. We listened until the record was finished. He stood up and took the needle from the record. He turned the power off. He said:

"Sick, huh?"

"Total."

"The fuck took you so long?"

"Ran into Donny."

"What, in jail?"

"Thought you were eating a sandwich."

"That was hours ago, let's roll, my parents will be home any second, and Clay is waiting."

That wasn't hours ago, it was ten minutes, and even if his parents were to come home it wouldn't matter, he just didn't want to talk to them. He liked drama.

When we got in his car I had to slam the door to close it. He yelled at me. I yelled back and told him to fix his fucking door. We didn't talk for five minutes because of it. Then he bummed a smoke and everything was fine.

Clayton was waiting for us when we got to his house. We bypassed the bentonite plant and went in through the back way. I got out and put the seat forward so he could get into the back. I pushed the seat back and got in. I slammed the door. I got yelled at. I said nothing.

The drive to the pits was quite pleasant. We bypassed town completely. We took a left just after the Mormon church and got on Highway 20, which was Bighorn Avenue, which was Main Street, and headed east. The sprinklers from the fields created a cool air. We drove with the windows rolled down. The air smelled of alfalfa and horseshit. When we slowed down to take a right I heard a donkey bray. The road became dusty. We rolled the windows up.

꧁꧂

The pits were what they sound like, a bunch of pits. A bunch of steep hills to ride your motorcycle up and down. Public land to devastate. A place to test new tires. To smoke pot. To place oil derricks. To shoot rabbits. To have bonfires and keggers. A place to avoid cops outside the city limits. A place almost lawless. Hidden from the world, but well known. A place for teenagers. A sanctuary.

When we got to the pits we pulled into what was essentially the parking lot. Because we were in a car we couldn't go much further. The hills were too steep. He parked and we got out. I slammed the door and got yelled at. It was early evening now. The air was cooling down. Rabbits darted from sagebrush to sagebrush. The wires from the telephone poles that ran next to the road made chirping noises. There was a derrick sucking oil from the ground. Justin went to the trunk of his car and opened it. He said:

"Shit." We came over and looked.

"What's up?"

"Thought my .22 was in here, where the hell did I put it?"

"What's that!"

"What, the twelve'er?"

"Well, yeah."

"Been there for a while, prolly skunky as shit."

"So what! Break it out!"

Turns out his dad had borrowed the car because he couldn't use his own on account of his third DUI and he had forgotten all about it. The beer was hot and skunky, but it was beer. We stood there with the trunk open drinking the beer. Clayton put his beer on the fender and took out his pipe and packed a bowl. He passed it around. I got high immediately. I declined the second round and got called a pussy, I took another hit. Before long I was stoned as a goat and drinking hot beer with a smirk on my face. Nobody said anything. The chirping from the telephone wire became intense. I giggled because of it. Then the derrick pumping the ground. So sexual. Then the rabbits running from sagebrush to sagebrush. So intense. Then silence and paranoia. Then the sound of motorcycles we hadn't noticed before. Then someone said we should go check it out. I grabbed the twelve-pack and Justin slammed the trunk shut.

The hill was as steep as the business side of silage, and just as crumbly. Luckily there were clumps of grass to grab onto. The three of us laughed hysterically at how difficult it was. I fell twice and slid at least six feet managing to hold on to the twelve-pack. By the time we got to the top we were covered in dirt. We looked back down at the path we had taken and laughed. There was a trail just to our left. Clayton spit off the edge.

I put the twelve-pack down and took out a cigarette. We all took out a cigarette. I lit mine and bent down. I took out beers. The beers foamed over when we opened them. We stood there drinking hot beers and smoking cigarettes. We could hear the motorcycles but we still couldn't see them. We decided to finish the beers and to leave the rest behind. I hid them under a sagebrush. It took us five minutes to finish the beers. Hot beer hurts your mouth. We crushed the empty cans and threw them over the edge of the hill, like we were skipping rocks into a lake of air. Mine went the furthest. Nobody was impressed but me.

We walked over to the pit where the motorcycle sounds were coming from. We stopped on the edge of the pit. We looked down. There was a black truck with a single wheel ramp resting on the gate. We knew who it was, of course, Clayton told me to go back and get the beer. I did. When I came back they were both sitting down on the edge of the pit watching as our friend Matt tried his best to get to the top of the pit. Both of them kept saying:

"He ain't gonna make it, he ain't gonna make it, ohh!" every time he got to the top and had to turn around because he didn't make it.

I sat down next to them and handed out beers. The sun was starting to set. We were facing west. The beers were lukewarm by now. The town lay in front of us. Fields of things green. Stretching out until more badlands. Then mountains. So forever. So boring. Such a stupid sunset. I could have puked. I didn't though, because Matt almost made it to the top! But he didn't.

We sat there watching until he gave up. It got too dark. Clayton packed another bowl and passed it around as Matt loaded his motorcycle back into the bed of his truck. He drove away. We drank the last three beers watching the sunset, irritated by the beauty. Justin said, fuck this, and stood up to piss. I did too. Then Clayton. We all pissed on sagebrush. The hill going back to the car was just as steep as it was when we were coming up. We slid down on our asses. We had a blast about it. Nothing but laughter. Justin made us dust ourselves off before we got in his car. I got in the back. Clayton got yelled at for slamming the door when he got in. The dude was relentless.

As we started driving Clayton put a tape in. He put the car in gear and gunned it. The car fishtailed. We all looked out the back and laughed at the dust cloud he created. He shifted into second gear. The car stayed in the same spot. The cloud got bigger. We all laughed harder. When it got too dusty he stopped pushing on the gas and crept onto the road. He turned the tape deck up.

When we got to the top of town I asked to be let out. I would walk down the hill. Justin pulled over. I got out. They took a right taking the back road to W. They peeled out as they drove away, both of their hands thrust out their windows, flipping me the bird.

The walk into town was pleasant. It was all downhill. I took a right at the campground and crossed the canal. The bridge was just a wooden plank that had been there since as long as I could remember. The canal smelled like dirt and crawdads. The water rubbed along the reeds that grew on the bank. The sound had more personality than what was the reality. The canal was quite boring and lazy. It fed the fields is all. A mere function of a farming community. All summer it ran, busy, busy, busy. And in the winter, just a gaping icy gash in the landscape.

I crossed the canal and took a left. The road was lined with Russian olive trees. There were fields of sugar beets beyond the trees. I was planning to follow the canal road until I got to the gas station by my house, but by the time I got to the first paved road my shoes were so stuck with thorns that I gave up. Goat heads, that's what they were called, the thorns. I spent a good minute kicking the pavement knocking the thorns out. It felt like I was wearing cleats.

The fields had given way to a patch of unkempt land that belonged to the city. It was overrun by prairie dogs. The sound of me kicking the pavement alarmed their town. I couldn't see them, but I knew that their lookouts were standing up. They were chirping at me. Or chirping because of me. They found me dangerous. I gave them no notice. I walked on.

All the houses I passed were duplexes. All of them had their porch lights on. Their curtains were closed. I could see the blue light of televisions on the second floor of nearly every one of them. That is where the living rooms were. A dog barked. Then another dog barked. I lit a cigarette. This part of town always made me nervous. It was where the teachers lived. It was also where I grew up. I knew every inch of it. I knew the alleys and the gutters. The places where if it rained during the day you would wipe out on your bike if you turned too fast. I knew which kids had what basement bedrooms, because for some reason the kids always got the basement bedrooms. I knew the cul de sacs. I knew which fathers secretly smoked, and which ones drank too much. The windows you could peep in if you wanted to see someone's mom naked. I knew the hedges and the fences. What the dogs looked like. Which one would bark when you walked by. I knew the trucks and the cars. The schedules of the parents. People's jobs and proclivities. There wasn't anything I didn't know. And they knew this too, all of them. And also, about me.

I walked on, smoking. I was trying to keep a low profile. I walked under a streetlight. I hid my cigarette. I looked around to see if anyone was watching. As far as I could tell nobody saw me. I walked another two blocks and then I was safe. Traffic. People thinking vague indifferent thoughts. Maybe heading to the A&W to get a hamburger, or heading to Greybull for reasons unknown, maybe to check out the Basin A&W, which puts cheese on their Coney Dog, can you imagine? Cheese on a Coney Dog?

I crossed the street when the traffic died down. I didn't

want to go home, but I had nowhere else to go. I took the alley by Shaky Joe's house and took as much time as my teenaged body would let me, which wasn't much.

The light from the garage was on. This meant my dad was working. I loved my dad, but he and I had very different ideas about the way things should be. I did, however, have a fascination with his taxidermy. With the way he treated animals. The bodies and the heads. I had watched him skin countless elk, deer, and antelope dangling like bats bleeding out the noses onto concrete, their blank black eyes reflecting the abysmal beauty of death, the smell of sagebrush and wool, the sound of a hacksaw on bone, and flies. Black flies. And the sound of salt being dumped on skin and rubbed in, sucking the moisture out. It was an art form.

I watched him skin heads too. Trial by error, boiling the heads too long until they became rubbery. Bleaching them in peroxide until they became brittle. Gluing the teeth back in at four in the morning watching pornography, because you got to watch something when you are gluing in teeth. He bought so much peroxide the government paid attention. They put him on a list. My father was an artist.

The radio was on. The radio was always on, he never turned it off. The station was country. Modern country. I knocked and went in. He was shaking an antelope's head loose of beetles. The nice thing about antelope is that their horns are basically hair, or fingernails, so you can take them off and glue them back on later. The garage smelled like death. I took a moment to adjust. I was used to it though. I watched him for a while saying nothing. He kept working in silence.

He had removed all the teeth from the head. They were in plastic cup on one of the shelves above the freezer. The bugs had removed all but a few black lines of muscle from the skull. He shut the freezer lid and put the head on top. I said:

"Whose is that?"

"Keiser's."

"Looks good."

"Yeah, for some reason they won't finish it, gonna have to scrape it."

"That's too bad."

"Yeah."

"Ok, hitting the sack."

I smelled like death as I walked into the house. My youngest brother was in the kitchen putting his dirty clothes in the bin by the washer and dryer. He was in his underwear. He was still wet from a bath. He told me p.u. and ran away. I kicked at him, but I didn't mean any harm, I was glad to see him. I walked into the living room and said hi to my mom. She said "hi honey, where have you been?"

I told her the pits and went into the bathroom.

My younger brother was in the bath playing with toys. He ignored me. I took a piss and flushed the toilet. I brushed my teeth. I went out to the living room again and said goodnight to my mom. She asked me if I was hungry. I said I wasn't, I'm tired. She said goodnight. I went into the bedroom and shut the door. I took my clothes off and got in bed. My youngest brother was lying in his own bed. The light was off. There was the sound of crickets from outside. The street light on the corner. The wallpaper covered in mold.

My youngest brother talked about birds until we both fell asleep.

In the morning my mom woke me up. As I was eating a piece of pizza I had cooked in the microwave for breakfast and drinking a cup of coffee the phone rang. It was my boss. He told me there was no work that day. I told him that was ok, and I was done working for the summer. He told me he was sorry to hear it and to call him if I changed my mind. I asked about getting my last check. He said he would drop it off later that day, or tomorrow. I said thanks. He said yep and hung up. My mom was looking at me as I hung up the phone. She said:

"Did you just quit your job?"

"He said he didn't need me today."

"Yeah, but what are you going to do for the rest of the summer?"

"I don't know."

"What do you mean you don't know?"

"I don't know, I'm tired, I'm going back to bed."

"No, huh-uh, let's talk about this."

"Mom!"

"Don't mom me, this is serious, you can't not work."

"But I hate it! I hate it so much, it makes me miserable."

"Well, join the club."

"But mom."

"Listen, honey, it's how it is. There's no way around it, I hate my job too."

"Yeah but that's you."

"You're impossible, what? You got another option all the sudden?"

"I don't know, maybe! There's something, I'm sure of it."

"Well let me know when you figure it out, I'll bake you a cake."

"You're the worst! I'm going back to bed."

"Yeah?"

"Yeah."

I went into the room I shared with my two brothers and slammed the door. They woke up, but neither of them said anything. I stripped off my clothes and got into bed. I could hear my mom slamming drawers in the living room. She was upset. The sun was coming through the window next to my bed. There was a swath of heat against my legs. It felt nice. Before long I was asleep.

When I woke up both my brothers were gone. I had a hard on. I masturbated. I thought about the woman behind the counter of the Mini Mart. She wore tight pants and had a nice voice. I used a dirty sock to clean up. I hid it under my pillow.

I got up and went into the living room. I turned the television on. There was nothing worth watching so I turned it off. I got bored. I went to the telephone and dialed Justin's number. Nobody answered. I hung up the phone.

I thought I should go out, so I got dressed. I went out the back door and took a left at the alley. Almost when I got to the street there was a noise in a freestanding garage. I knew who it was. I knocked on the door. I went in. Donny, the guy with the clever way of huffing gas while cruising Main, the guy from the dumpster wearing handcuffs, was sitting on a couch with his friend Eddy. I said hi.

They were smoking pot. They offered it to me. I declined. He gave me some wisdom:

"See this? Fucking shit bro, check it out. Man, you use a Brillo pad for a screen, like really, and then it just burns out. Fucking shit, just rip another hunk off and cram it in!"

I nodded and smiled. I couldn't handle the scene, so I left.

I didn't know what to do, so I walked to the Mini Mart. The woman I had just masturbated about was cleaning up the gas stalls. I said hi and went to the pay phone. I picked up the receiver and dialed 1-800-HOT-BOYS. I listened to the message and laughed. I hung up the phone.

I dug a quarter out of my pocket and picked up the receiver again. I put the quarter in the slot. I dialed Justin again. This time he picked up:

"Hello."

"There you are, what are you doing?"

"Oh hey, just got home."

"Fucking bored."

"Where you at?"

"Mini Mart, come get me."

"Yeah, ok."

I stood there waiting. I watched the girl with the tight pants and nice voice change the garbage can trash. There was a song in my head.

When Justin showed up I got into his car. I had to slam the door in order to shut it. He yelled at me. "Don't slam my fucking door."

The dude was relentless. I said sorry. I didn't mean it.

We drove out West River Road and went to the hanging bridge. We took the access road and parked beside the river. We got out of the car. The air was filled with flies. It smelled like mustard and lipstick. I lit a cigarette and kicked a rock and slammed the door. Justin yelled at me. The dude was relentless.

We went under the bridge. There was graffiti on its walls. The word turds was prevalent, as well as the word butt. Justin took out his one hitter and packed it. He smoked it. He packed it again and handed it to me. I handed him my cigarette. I lit the pipe and was immediately stoned. I saw a duck.

The next few minutes drifted by in silence. The rolling of the river and the roiled action of the cottonwood leaves. I probably would have enjoyed it if I didn't hate it so much. The place gave me the creeps.

We stood there underneath the bridge until it got boring. The duck flew away. We got back into the car. We headed back towards town. The idea was to go get Clayton and talk about the weekend, about camping. That was the idea at least.

Nobody was home when we got to his place. Not even the dog. We let ourselves in and went into the basement. We thought briefly about just waiting for him to show up, but there was no telling when he might get back. We went outside and stood by the car contemplating our next move. We could hear the dump trucks being loaded with bentonite. The traffic on the highway. We both lit cigarettes. When we were about to give up completely he pulled into the dirt lot that was his driveway. He was driving his mother's white Toyota pickup truck. The dog was in the back. When he stopped the dog jumped out and ran up to me, licking my hand. I petted its head. It wagged its tail. Clayton got out as well. He had a cigarette in his mouth. His hair was white and cut short, like something from a roman statue. He had a beard. The beard was slightly red. He had a smile on his face that I could never tell what it meant. It was half smirk and half nervousness. He asked us what we were up to. Justin said:

"This goober just quit his job, want to go camping tomorrow?"

"Why not go right now?"

"Yeah, sure, why not?"

"Yeah, ok," I said.

"Let me get my things, c'mon Tony!"

We followed him and his dog back inside. We watched him pack some clothes into a bag. He found his sleeping bag and threw it on the ground next to the bag. He sat down on his bed and loaded the bong. He took a rip and handed it to Justin. He took a rip while standing up. He handed it to me. I did the same. My rip cashed it. I set the bong on top of his dresser.

We went upstairs to the kitchen. Clayton opened his refrigerator and took out some tortillas and cheese slices and some sliced turkey and a bottle of ranch dressing. He put it in his bag. He whistled for Tony. The dog came up the stairs and went outside through the door he was holding open. He said, hold on I should write a note. He went into the living room and wrote a note for his mom. Went camping. Be home Sunday. Then we left.

My house was much of the exact same, except the note I left had my name at the bottom. I was glad my dad wasn't around to yell at me for quitting my job. I'm sure he hadn't talked to my mom yet, but I would have felt obligated to tell him. I threw my stuff in the trunk of the car and got back in. We drove off.

Justin's house was a little bit different, we decided we should take the work van parked out front of his house. Which meant he needed to call his dad. Which meant me and Clayton stood outside on the sidewalk smoking for long enough to grow impatient. We were quite relieved when he showed back up with his bags and the van keys.

On our way out of town we stopped to get gas. Clayton used his brothers I.D. to buy us beer. I bought jerky and several packs of cigarettes. After that we were on the road.

꧁❀꧂

The drive to the mountains took us through Tensleep and into Tensleep Canyon. We pulled in off the highway next to a sign that said Leigh Creek Campground. We were supposed to put money in the fee box before we entered, but there was an idea we might go up to the higher campgrounds on the Old Highway which were free sites.

We drove around looking around, looking for anybody we knew. There was mostly nobody there. The sites that were taken were mostly Nebraska and Dakota plates. We drove to the furthest site closest to the entrance to the Old Highway and took our chances on not paying. The road had been closed due to a high fire danger.

We set up camp, which consisted of us standing next to the van drinking beer. Clayton took out his pipe and loaded a bowl. He passed it around. The mosquitoes were terrible. We talked briefly about heading up to the higher campground by Meadowlark where it would be cooler and have fewer bugs. The conversation got dropped and we stood there with idiot grins on our faces. Holding beers. Kind of looking at each other. Stoned as goats.

A truck pulled up. What happened next is up for debate. There was a sound of a thwack a ding and a whack. I guess the debate is about the order. Whoever was in that truck shot at us with a BB gun. The BB either hit my hand and bounced up hitting Justin, in the tooth, or hit his tooth and reflected, hitting my hand. Either way we stood there stunned and unable to comprehend what happened. The truck had peeled off, laughing. We could hear they were kids like us. We stood there too stoned to move quickly. Then Justin said:

"What the hell was that? They got my tooth, you're bleeding!"

I looked down at my hand. I was in fact bleeding. Before anyone could think we were in the van speeding towards the campground entrance. Clayton was in the passenger seat loading his pistol. I was kneeling in between the two front seats holding onto the headrests. Justin was driving with a focus unblinking.

By the time we got to the entrance of the campground they were long gone. This was for the best. Not that we would have used the gun, but shit like this did tend to get ugly. For some reason there was a rivalry between each town. Tensleep was rivals with W, and W was rivals with Thermopolis, everybody hated Cody and Powell wasn't worth the time. And nobody liked county nine. They were terrible drivers. Nothing ever really happened except fist fights, but there was usually booze involved, so things got kind of bloody, and also generations of feuding. The Bowers versus the Millers, the Whites versus the Carters and such.

There was no reason to chase them into town so we turned around and went back to our camp. Justin's tooth wasn't broken and my hand had stopped bleeding.

We went back to drinking beer and standing around. Eventually we built a fire. Justin had brought a skillet and bacon and potatoes and eggs. This would be dinner. The fire pit had a metal ring and a grill. When the initial logs died down and burned red he put the skillet on the grill and dumped the entire package of bacon in it. It sizzled. He cut the potatoes into cubes on the picnic table next to the fire pit. He was careful to avoid the bird shit. He threw the potatoes on top of the bacon. He stirred everything with a knife. The sun went away and the day cooled down. It was still early, but we were in the mountains. We watched the fire as the daylight disappeared. It got cold enough that we all put on sweaters. Justin added black pepper to the potatoes and bacon.

꧁꧂

By the time the potatoes were done we had eaten all the bacon. We decided to leave the eggs for breakfast and ate the potatoes out of the skillet as they cooked. Justin put the skillet on the picnic table and covered it with two pieces of firewood so the magpies wouldn't get at it. He would use the grease for the eggs.

Because dinner was finished we could get a proper fire going. Whoever had camped there before had left a huge stack of firewood. Maybe half a cord. Why you would need that much wood for a couple days of camping was always a source of amusement, especially considering you could walk into the trees just beyond the camp and get way more than enough. And not only that, but most people that camped here used gas to cook with, it was like using a blowtorch to light your smoke. Fucking tourists.

As the fire grew brighter the camp became isolated. The stars disappeared. The trees began to dance around us. We could see each other. Drinking beer and staring at the flames. We smoked more pot and cigarettes. Every so often somebody would get up and go piss just on the edge of the firelight. Nobody said much of anything. When we spoke it wasn't of much consequence. Hand me a beer. Fuck, I am out of smokes, cough it up. I'm hitting the sack.

Justin and Clayton hit the sack at the same time. They were sleeping in the van. My plan was to sleep next to the fire. They threw my sleeping bag at me as they laid their own down on the floor of the van. I suppose they were being nice, but I think they just didn't want to be disturbed when I was going to bed. Whoever threw it said, here you go fucker, and laughed. I said thanks and picked it up off the ground and dusted it off. I put it on top of the picnic table. I sat down next to the fire again.

There was a nice silence as I watched the wood turn into coals. The moon rose above the canyon walls, making things white. A breeze caused by the hot air of the canyon floor rushing towards the top of the canyon. The sound of the creek rushing to lower ground. The smell of pine and sage and smoke. The weird birds of the night.

I stared at the fire until the coals made me hallucinate. I decided I was either drunk or stoned and should probably go to bed. I went to the edge of the camp and took a piss. I came back. I put my sleeping bag on the ground next to the fire and took my shoes off. I got into the bag. I didn't have a pillow. I reached down and grabbed one of my shoes. I put it under my head. I stared up at the sky.

The moon was bright but quickly disappeared when it got to the other edge of the canyon. The fire was nothing but coals. The sky looked like white chalk scraped against black butcher paper. I watched satellites race against the earth until I fell asleep.

It was raining in the morning. I moved my operation to under the picnic table. I was dry, but there were a lot of bugs. I hid my head inside of my sleeping bag. I forgot to bring my shoes with me, so they were both wet when I finally got up. The rain didn't last long, but it soaked everything that was left out. The sun eventually came out and made everything unbearably hot. I was draping my sleeping bag over the picnic table when Justin opened the door of the van. He lit a cigarette and asked me why I hadn't lit the fire. I asked him the same, he said:

"Shit, did it rain?"

"What's it look like?"

"Fuck you, light the fire."

"I'm drying my bag."

"Want breakfast?"

"You're a fucking dick."

"A dick that has to pee," he disappeared into the bushes.

Clayton emerged from the van. He lit a cigarette. He coughed. He coughed a lot. He loved smoking. He said:

"Who's a dick?"

"Who do you think?"

"Did it rain? Why ain't the fire going?" I shook my head. He went off and pissed.

Lighting the fire took two seconds. Most of the wood was still dry. I used some napkins I found in the van as kindling. It wasn't long before the oil left in the skillet was smoking and all twelve eggs from the carton were being stirred by a small branch that Justin had broken off from a tree that was green.

The eggs were great. Quite tasty. We ate them out of the skillet sitting on the picnic table. They were followed by a tightly packed bowl of weed and a warm beer. A cigarette and a decision to go for a hike.

The hike was easy at first. We took the Old Highway up past the switchbacks, but then we veered off. It became nearly vertical at this point. We brought nothing with us except cigarettes. We got about half a mile up before we were dying of thirst. We sat down and stared across the canyon. We were sitting on a cliff and somebody kicked a rock. We watched it roll all the way to the creek bed, knocking things down as it went. Things like trees. We found this glorious. The next thing that happened we were looking for the biggest boulders we could find. Anything we were strong enough to roll, we watched roll down into the creek, destroying everything in its path, hoping nobody was fishing down there.

This went on until we ran out of boulders we could move. We made our way back down to the campground. When we got to the camp something felt like it was missing. Clayton said something about Big Piney. Movement sounded nice, so we packed up everything and got back in the van. Somebody asked if we should take some of the wood. Somebody else said no, there will be some there.

This was probably true.

✾

Big Piney was quite the distance. A five-hour drive in fact. Clayton had heard there was a festival there. A bunch of hippies making love, is what he called it. It sounded like an orgy. An orgy sounded nice. When we got to Tensleep we pulled into the Little Indian to get some gas. I gave Justin ten of my last thirteen dollars to pay for gas. I went inside and ordered a cheeseburger from the counter. All three of us did. It was a tradition to get a hamburger here when coming down from the mountain. Technically we weren't coming down from the mountain, we were only coming from the lower fork, but still, we were going the opposite way through town.

The next thirty minutes for me were rough. First of all I wasn't where I told my parents I was supposed to be anymore. Second, I was heading towards a town three hundred miles from where I was supposed to be. Third, we were about to drive back through town, where anybody and everybody I knew would see us, and could easily tell my mom and dad.

The cheeseburger felt like an anchor in my guts. I begged them to take the back roads through town. They laughed at me. Justin took Main just to be an asshole.

I laid down in the back of the van as we went through town. Not that anyone could see inside anyway, the van had no windows on its sides. I did it out of nervousness. The two stoplights in town were murder. I could feel the eyes of society upon me. Making notice. Like a snake made of gossip ready to bite me in the ass. I kept my eyes closed, listening to every whimper and creak. When we crossed the train tracks I felt it in the wheels. We were clear, or I guess, I was clear, as far as I could tell. The van went from town speed to highway speed and I sat up.

The road out of town hugged the river. It went up a hill and opened the expanse of the landscape on your eyes like a dirty diaper filled with diarrhea spilling on your lap. Beautiful like a baby but disgusting too. Sweet and apparent.

We passed the Boys School and Gooseberry. Passed the longest continuous single curve of train track in North America. Passed into the oblivion that separates towns from towns in Wyoming. This nothing. This nothing but empty space. This thing that if you could turn your head around fast enough and looked back at the everything that you are, you would die, and the shock of it would bring you back into existence. Nothing. Boredom.

This boring landscape spread into oblivion. Hills that led into hills that led into mountains that led into the sunset. We were heading south so the sun was on our right. Rabbits ran across the road. Justin tried to run them over. We passed farms and ranches. Access roads and barns. We smoked pot and cigarettes.

When we got to Thermopolis Justin told us to keep our cool. He was stoned. Luckily the town only had one traffic light. We made it through without incident. Before anybody could panic we were back on the highway. Five minutes later we were in the canyon.

The canyon was easier this time. Going up is less terrifying than coming down. It was scary enough though for Justin to drive seriously. When we got to the dam we talked about jumping off of it. They were still impressed I had had the balls to do it, meaning being the first to do it.

When we got past the dam the landscape opened up again like a turbulent baby, but it was dusk now. The landscape disappeared. The sky turned slowly black. Soon it was highway and stars. Headlights.

When we got to Shoshone we took a right. We could have gone left, but we didn't. This was the back roads version of the state. We were in danger. We were high, had weed, had beer, underage and aimless.

When we got to Riverton we cruised right through.

They had two traffic lights, but because we were in a work van we didn't need to worry. Riverton was on the reservation. Racism made us invisible.

When we got to Lander we pulled over in the parking lot of a hotel. Clayton and I got out of the van with a hose and plastic five-gallon gas jug. Justin stayed in the drivers seat with the engine running. It took a while to find a car that didn't have a screen that kept us from sticking the hose in, but when we did Clayton blew twice and sucked once. The gas poured out.

It took three minutes to do this. We could tell nobody was watching. We took the gas can back to the van and poured it in the tank. We went back and did it again.

This time when the jug was almost full the hose made a sucking noise, like a straw at the bottom of a milkshake. We laughed. We had sucked it dry. Or we supposed. We ran back to the van and poured it in the tank. We hopped in the van. Justin crept out of the parking lot so as to not make any noise. When he got to the main road he peeled out like an idiot. The van stunk of gas. We all laughed without control. We left the windows down.

The next three hours in the van were like chewing wool. It was moist but you couldn't absorb it. I fell asleep a few times. Then Clayton did. Then he traded me seats in the front and I smoked cigarettes out the window. Then he woke up and Justin pulled the van over so Clayton could drive. Then Justin got in the back, and Clayton and I listened to the radio.

The moon came up and the world looked pretty easy. I was far enough from my parents to think about whether they were mad at me or not, and the idea of a destination, any destination, seemed so vague that I could eat the bitterness of the horizon like the peel of an orange. As stupid as they were, things looked pretty good.

By the time we got to Piney Pass it was two in the morning. We took it slow and deliberate. Clayton and I smoked a bowl as Justin slept in back. When we got to the other side we pulled over. He said he needed to sleep. I agreed. We took our sleeping bags out and laid down in the back of the van. Justin woke up briefly and said he needed some water. He farted and went back to sleep. We laughed and went to sleep ourselves.

In the morning the sun made the van uncomfortable. Justin had gotten up and was drinking a beer, he still wanted water and he also wanted to know where we were at. Clayton said:

"We're outside of Pindale, we can get water there."

"How far?" he yawned.

"I don't fucking know, just drive, we're close, what the hell do you care?"

"Gas, bitch tits."

"It doesn't matter either fucking way, either we run out of gas or you leave me the fuck alone."

"Fuck you."

We made it to town just barely. The gas was completely gone. I rode shotgun as Clayton slept in the back and Justin fumed as he drove. I really don't know why he expected a full tank of gas, but his feelings were definitely hurt.

Pinedale was puny. There was just one gas station and that was it. We bought gas and asked for directions to Big Piney. The guy running the place told us with a warning about the hippies and the orgies that were about to happen there. We thanked him like teenagers. We peeled out shooting rocks at him. He shook his head and went back inside.

Ten miles down the road there was a turn off. There was a sign that said Big Piney. We took it. The road was rough but passable. When we got to where we thought we were going there was a meadow and a clearing. There was two other vans. Nothing else. We parked the van. We gathered our things and walked towards what looked like a campfire.

The campfire wasn't a campfire.

The hippies had dug a heart into the ground. They had filled it with sage and were burning it in order to purify the communal hearth. That's what they called it, the communal hearth. The leader of the group was a man in his forties who called himself Laser Beam X Ray. He was skinny and short, naked from the waist up. He was deeply tanned and called us brothers. He said:

"Welcome brothers, sorry I haven't had a chance to clean up." He pretended to be embarrassed. The six other hippies laughed at his joke, I guess he was treating the wilderness as his house and he hadn't had a chance to clean up his house, I guess. We just stared at him. "Just put your things in the guest bedroom." He pointed to a spot away from the heart pit. We shrugged and took our stuff over to a spot that looked level. We all returned holding a warm beer in our hands. He told us we couldn't drink those here. We just stared at him. Justin asked him what's up with the pit. He said:

"Seriously, this is a dry ceremony, your alcohol is ruining the vibe."

"Well, I'm pretty sure we're on public land, and pretty sure you can suck a fat dreadlock needle dick." That was Clayton talking, the one with the beard. He loved this shit.

"Don't call me that," he was immediately on the verge of tears. One of his cronies stepped in.

"It's ok Laze, I got this, look guys we don't want any trouble, maybe you can go over there and drink your beers, we're just trying to bless this communal hearth, then you are more than welcome to join us." Justin looked at us. We both shrugged.

"Whatever."

We took our beers and walked back to our stuff and started to set up camp.

We didn't have a tent, but we did have a tarp. We stretched it out and put our sleeping bags and beer on it. Camp was set up. Clayton got the cold cuts and tortillas and sliced cheese and ranch dressing out. We all made ourselves what was known as a food stamp burrito, because it was something only poor people would eat. There was probably something racist involved too, but I still couldn't tell you what. Afterwards I laid down on my sleeping bag and watched the clouds. I ended up falling asleep. When I woke Justin and Clayton were gone and there were about twenty more people at the heart pit.

I lit a cigarette and walked over. My friends were nowhere to be seen. The heart pit was now an actual fire. There were other fires too. People were cooking things in large pots. The air smelled like beans. I looked around for a while and then made my way toward the van. I found the two sitting in the back with the doors open smoking pot and listening to music. The van was running. I said what's up and they handed me the pipe. I took a hit and handed it back. The parking lot was now filled with vehicles. Mostly out of state plates. Not mostly, ours was the only Wyoming plate in the lot. I sat down on the bumper smoking my cigarette watching more and more cars drive in. Mostly European vans with plates like Oregon and California and Minnesota and Colorado. The people would park and get out of the vehicle and smell the fresh air like it was some sort of tonic. Stretch and unload their shit. They all did this. They all called us brothers as they walked by on the way to the heart pit carrying their backpacks and water bottles.

Dusk rolled in and the temperature dropped. We decided to go get our sweaters from our things. When we got to our camp we were completely surrounded by tents. The place smelled of patchouli and body odor. We could hear people having sex. The smell of beans was stronger than before. We wondered if the hippies were going to share. We decided to drink a beer and watch. When the sun finally went down there was a bell that rang. People started to flock towards the heart pit. We decided this meant it was time to eat. We followed the flock.

The crowd gathered around the heart pit, the man called Laser Beam X Ray stood on an upturned log and made a speech. He said something about the earth and giving what you get and some other stuff that made everybody cheer. When he was finished the crowd lined up in a row next to a tent that had been erected. We got in line.

The food was beans with cumin, rice with cumin and raisins, and something that was probably yogurt. It wasn't half bad. We got into the habit of calling everybody brother. We ate standing up next to the heart pit, which was now a bonfire pit. The gathering became peaceful. There were high spirits. This was supposed to be the biggest one yet we kept hearing. People kept disappearing to hump in their tents. We did too, but not to hump in our tent, but to smoke pot and drink beer on our tarp. We waited for the orgy to happen. The orgy never happened. When the drums came out and people started dancing like natives. I slipped away and hit the sack.

It took a while to find a place to take a piss and brush my teeth before I went to bed. There were now over a hundred hippies sprawled out on the grass. When I got back to our camp I took off my shoes and sweater and climbed in the sack. The tarp crinkled as I made myself comfortable. I put my sweater under my head and stared at the stars.

The universe played like a movie in my eyes. I was drunk and stoned and spinning. The drums being whacked and the bonfire glowing in my periphery. The sound of sex in tents. I closed my eyes and fell asleep.

The morning was hot. I woke up sweating in my sleeping bag. I unzipped it and unleashed the smell of campfire smoke and sweat and two days of unwashed body. I was dehydrated. I looked around for water. I only found our dwindled supply of warm beer. I cracked one open. It tasted like a skunks ass dipped in formaldehyde.

Justin and Clayton had showed up at some point during the night. They were still asleep on the tarp. Justin was lying on top of his bag with his pants down around his knees. His tight white underwear were still on though. Thankfully. He did however have an erection that was moist at the tip. He must not have gotten laid.

Clayton, however was lying perpendicular to us, half on and half off the tarp. His head was inside his bag. My movement must have woke him up. He curled into a ball and farted. Then he laughed. Then he must have fallen back to sleep because I could hear him snoring.

I stood up and made my way toward the trees. I felt like I was navigating a war camp after a battle. Everything was quiet but brutal. People were sprawled out, some lying face down in the grass, others smoking and cooking coffee or tea in hushed little circles around butane stoves, still others moaning like badgers inside their tents. The smell was unfriendly. There was naked skin and pubic hair everywhere.

I had to step over multiple lifeless bodies to get to the edge of the forest. I stepped behind a tree and took a leak. I made my way back and sat down on my sleeping bag. I drank the rest of my horrible beer and put my shoes on. I lit a smoke and walked down to the heart pit.

The pit was smoking. There were a few people staring at it, looking dazed. They were sitting down. They didn't bother looking up at me as I approached. I said nothing. They said even less. I walked on.

The mess tents were a mess. Pots were tipped over and camp robber birds were going to town on the scraps of food that had been left behind. I kept walking.

I wanted some water. I went to the van and discovered it was locked. The parking lot was a fit of activity. There were new arrivals by the handful, maybe the dozens. I saw a vanload of people unloading jugs of water. I went over and begged a couple of gulps please. Sure thing brother. The water was warm but refreshing. I walked down the road towards the turn off. There was a constant line of cars coming into the parking lot. I turned around and went back to our camp.

When I got to the tarp Justin and Clayton were awake

and sitting up. They were smoking a bowl. I sat down. They handed me the pipe. I took it. I handed it back. One of them handed me a beer. I opened it. I took a drink and made a face. I said:

"Jesus, there's a fucking shitload more coming in just now, I think we should get the hell out of here."

"You ever find the shitter?"

"It's over there, you see that log?" They both looked. There was a log with ten people sitting down, taking a shit.

"Oh, hell no!"

"Yeah."

"Yeah, ok."

It took us all of five minutes to break camp. Clayton helped me fold the tarp as Justin put the supplies back in the plastic bag. We each crammed our sleeping bags back into their bags. There was nobody to say goodbye to so we just left.

As we were throwing our stuff into the back of the van a guy came up and watched us. Someone said:

"Hey man, what's up?"

"Hey brothers, how's the trip been?"

"Fine, I guess."

"I got some of that free love last night!" he was smiling.

"Well ain't that nice, oh hey, you want these? We couldn't drink them."

"Well hell yeah I do! What you guys leaving? This shit's just getting started!"

We ignored him until he went away. Those beers would be punishment enough. We got in the van and left.

It was an hour before we were going down the pass again. Justin was still tired so he traded me for the front seat. He laid down in the back and Clayton and I smoked pot and listened to music as the land in front of us became scary and beautiful. The roads became bendy and he started laughing as he drove. He whispered, check this out, and threw his head in a way that made me check out the back of the van. Justin was sleeping soundly, lying on his back. Peaceful. The next curve in the road Clayton gunned it and the van flew into a centripetal rage, Justin went rolling to the side, then the next corner was the opposite, and he rolled into the other side of the van. Clayton was laughing as he did this, I did too, I usually hated the way they bullied me, but this was actually funny. He kept doing it. Justin kept trying to get his bearings but he couldn't. Because he was asleep when this started he was seconds behind the action. Had he just laid down again he would have been fine, but he was resisting. This made it worse. It was a comedy. It was a lesson in being an asshole. This was the first time I had seen it from this vantage. I am certain it wasn't a sign of respect, it was only opportunity, but still, it was a damn good laugh. A little bit of a victory. A much needed victory.

The rest of the ride home was uneventful. Justin was sore for a while, but he got over it by the time we stopped at a gas station and had to buy all the gas himself because Clayton and I had no more money. He drove the rest of the way.

When we got to town he kicked me out at Main and Railroad. I stood there holding my sleeping bag watching them drive away wondering what the hell I was doing in this fucking town with these fucking assholes.

I walked towards the post office and took a right on Robertson. I wondered what I would tell my mom about the weekend when I got home. Whether I would tell her anything at all.

❧

Getting home was a simple matter of walking three blocks, crossing Fifteenth and walking another three blocks. I was home in no time. As I approached the house I could see a game of hacky sack was being played on the sidewalk. We had a large sidewalk because our house was so far inset from street. The house was a rental. I think the property line ended at the grass. The city maintained the sidewalk. My youngest brother got paid twenty dollars a month to mow the lawn, from the landlord. The sidewalk in front of the house was three times larger than most sidewalks.

The game of hacky sack excited me. Not the game itself, which was just kicking a sack of beans, but because it was my older brother and my oldest brother and some girl I had never met.

My oldest brother was back from college, well not college proper, but back from Powell where he went to college, from where he had stayed on for the summer to work at a lumberyard. I threw my sleeping bag on the lawn and joined the circle.

I was introduced to my brother's friend, her name was Mary. She was from two towns over. I said hi. I then said to my oldest brother:

"You grew out your hair." He had shoulder length hair and was wearing ripped jeans and a cardigan.

"Yep, how was camping?"

"Same-ol, you doing in town?"

"I don't know, thought I'd come say hi, got a couple days off. Heard you quit your job."

"Fucking mom."

"You gotta work though dude, what else ya gonna do?"

"I don't know, what do I care, fuck this shit hole."

"Yeah, well, dad's a little pissed."

"Good for him."

"Well, how's the bomber holding up?"

"Still sparking the solenoid, but it's running just fine, got it up to fifty like a week ago!"

"No shit!"

While this conversation went on we passed the bag of beans between us. My older brother did fancy tricks. He was actually good at the game. The rest of us just barely managed to pass it to somebody else. My two younger brothers were playing on the lawn. A weird game of tag involving a Frisbee. They were both very happy that we were all home together again. Like me, they missed my oldest brother.

I asked the girl how she knew my brother. She said:

"From college." That was it. I was instantly smitten. I asked my brother how long he was staying for. He said just the night. He had plans to stay in Greybull with Mary, and get back to Powell the next day.

That night the whole family had dinner together. My dad grilled venison on the back porch. My mom made a salad from her garden. My two younger brothers got so worked up that they passed out on the floor before bath time. My dad carried them to bed.

After that he ran himself a bath and disappeared. My older brother went downstairs and disappeared. Mary told my mom thank you for the dinner, and asked me if I wanted to come with her and my oldest brother. They were going out. I, of course, said yes.

Mary drove a silver Toyota Tercel. Stick. I got in the back seat, my oldest brother took shotgun. She was barely in second gear before we all had lighted cigarettes in our mouths. The windows were rolled down already. The radio was on.

She drove a few blocks and pulled into the groceries parking lot. She and my oldest brother got out. They told me to wait in the car. I already knew the drill. They were both twenty-one. They couldn't go through the drive-through with a minor in the car. When they came back they had a twelve-pack of Coors and a bottle of Seagrams. The whiskey was in a paper sack. Mary backed out of her parking spot and headed towards the hills.

Fifteen minutes later we were ten miles past the fair grounds. We took a right and drove up a hill that would kill a very dear friend of mine ten years later. She pulled the car over and we all got out. My oldest brother put the beer and the bottle on top of the hood. He broke the twelve-pack open and handed us both a beer. He took one for himself. He said:

"Man, this fucking shit hole." The stars were as bright as if god was poking holes in the sky because he was trying to look down on us, to see how we were doing. The air smelled of sage. Antelope were barking in the distance. It was terrifyingly ugly, how beautiful it was.

Nobody said anything for a while. Eventually my brother asked me:

"Why'd you quit your job? What's going on?"

"Why'd you go to college?"

"Seriously."

"Why'd you go to college Mary?"

"I don't know, why'd you quit your job?" she said.

"Fuck you guys!"

"I'm just sayin, you know you gotta work, fucking fact of life."

"Yeah, well."

"Well, dad's pissed."

"He can stay pissed. I'm sick of this shit, you got it easy, both of you, being at college, away from home."

"I'm at home for the summer." Mary laughed. "My dad is out of town though." She trailed off. She was the youngest of three sisters. Her mom had died from cancer when she was seventeen. At home. Her dad never got over it. Her older sisters ignored it. She was essentially alone.

"Well maybe I will hang out with Mary for the summer then." I said this to my oldest brother as a threat of idleness, but Mary liked the idea.

"There you go! I'll take care of this little shit, teach him the ropes," she said.

My brother laughed. She was serious though. I noticed, but my brother didn't, things were changing. I could feel it. He opened the bottle of whiskey. He took a drink and handed it to me. I took a drink and was immediately drunk. It felt nice. I handed the bottle to Mary as the moon broke the edge of the horizon. The ugly beauty was like a boot upon my neck. Insistent and brutal. Choking me out.

We had to creep all the way to town. The stupid cops liked to patrol the outskirts with their Keg Buster. Looking for kids drinking. Technically they couldn't go past the city limits, but they knew all of our drinking spots. All they had to do was wait for us to get back on the paved road and follow us to town, hoping we would fuck up. We always fucked up, and they were always there to notice.

Mary drove the speed limit with no exception. She was hyper-aware of the surroundings. There were no headlights in the rearview yet, but things tend to switch pretty quick.

When we dropped into town and took a left there was a new misery. We were in town now, so the other police that had nothing better to do, liked to sit and wait for us to fuck up. We didn't fuck up, but there were no back roads to take to get home, so Mary stoked her diligence, and me and my brother too.

We got home just fine. We even passed a police car without any hesitation. She parked in front of our house but on the other side of the street. We got out and crossed the street. Mary was talking loud and I told her she should be quiet and pointed to our parent's window. It was open. She put her hand on her mouth and pretended to be embarrassed. I couldn't help but laugh.

We snuck around the back of the house and went in through the back door. It was after midnight and nobody was up. I told them I was hitting the sack and went into the bathroom. I could hear them making food and drinking my dad's beer as I went to bed. My brothers were asleep as I took my clothes off. The moon was the only light in the room. There were crickets outside the windows.

When I woke in the morning both my brothers were gone. It was late but not too late, I could tell because my youngest brother was mowing the lawn. I took the moment of solitude to masturbate. I thought about my brother's friend. I felt dirty afterwards. I cleaned up with the sock I had under my pillow. I put it back and got out of bed.

Nobody was in the living room. Nobody was in the house as far as I could tell. I looked out the front door and saw that my brother's friend's car was no longer across the street. I went back into the living room and turned on the television. I went into the kitchen and looked into the refrigerator. There was a bunch of leftover tacos from the one taco place in town that was good. I put them on top of the counter which doubled as a dishwasher, all you had to do was connect it to the kitchen sink. I couldn't be in the house when it was running. It made me sick. The smell. But it wasn't running.

I put the thing of tacos on the counter and got a plate. I put three tacos on the plate and put them in the microwave. I hit the one-minute button. I turned around and got some coffee. The coffee pot was mostly always on. I went into the living room and put the coffee on the table in front of the couch. The microwave dinged. I went back to the kitchen and got the tacos. I grabbed a fork and sat down.

As I ate my tacos with a fork I watched the television. Nothing was on. I opened the newspaper that was sitting on the table. The front page was a load of horseshit and the vital statistics didn't mention anybody I knew had died. I flipped the page and read the police report. A friend of mine had been arrested for MIP and MIPT, minor in possession, and minor in possession of tobacco. I fucking hated the cops. And below this an ad for ninety-nine cent taco burgers at Taco Johns.

I loved taco burgers.

I took my plate back into the kitchen and opened the dishwasher. It was full of clean dishes. I closed it and put my dirty plate in the sink. I went outside and was assaulted by the sun as I walked down the porch steps. My youngest brother was still mowing the lawn. I smiled. He was so small behind that big mower. He tried so hard. I still don't know what his motivation was. I don't know, maybe he had a unique viewpoint, being the youngest, like he looking at the rest of us from some weird telescope and could see all of our faults, and was trying to make up for it. I waved at him. He waved back and kept pushing the mower.

I sat down on the steps and lit a cigarette. I was half way through when my oldest brother and my brother's friend pulled up upfront. They both got out of the car and approached me. My oldest brother said:

"Wanna go to Powell?"

"Fuck hell I do!"

"We're leaving now. Tell mom."

"Can't you? She'll just yell at me."

He looked at me and crinkled his eyes. It was a smile. "Sure, grab some clothes and your toothbrush."

I ran inside and packed a bag of random things. Random shirts. Random socks. A pair of pants that I had never ever worn. I grabbed my toothbrush and went into the living room. My oldest brother was talking on the phone with my mom. He said:

"Nah, it's alright...No, no, he'll stay with me, he needs this...look, I'll have him call you...ok...ok...yes, tonight, what do you mean? Ha! Ok, love ya." He hung up. He looked at me. "Call your mom."

I called my mom. She said:

"Hi, honey."

"Hi, mom"

"You will listen to your brother right?"

"Ok."

"You know you are special cargo?"

"Mom!"

"Don't mom me! Listen to your brother."

"I will mom."

"Good. Did you pack underwear?"

"Mom!"

"I love you."

I hung up. I went into the bedroom I shared with my brothers and grabbed some underwear out of the bin. Stupid mom, always looking out for me.

I was packed and ready when my oldest brother and his friend came into the living room. Ready? I nodded. We went out the front door. I waved again at my youngest brother still mowing the lawn. He waved back.

His waving stalled the motor. I felt bad. We threw our bags in the back of the Silver Toyota Tercel and got inside.

I watched my youngest brother yanking on the mower cord as we drove away. He couldn't get it started again. My guts felt like they were connected to that cord.

Luckily there was a small cloud of black smoke pouring out of the lawn mower as I lost sight. Otherwise I would have pictured him yanking that cord for hours.

He was without a doubt the sweetest person I knew.

Powell was roughly a two-hour drive from W. I sat in the back seat feeling excited and nervous. I'm sure I talked like a chatterbox the whole time, but I don't remember a single word that was said.

The hills and trees and sagebrush and gullies and ranches and farms and feedlots and highway came at us like plywood. I felt like we were riding a saw blade on a table saw, ripping the landscape in two. It felt like we were stationary. Like the world was coming to us, like we were blessed. Like we were ripping the world a new asshole. Tearing it asunder. Like we were carpenters. Carpenters with magnificent plans.

We took a left in Basin, the sneaky back road highway, avoiding my oldest brother's friend's hometown.

The highway was slower by ten miles an hour, but it circumvented Greybull and town, and also a huge chunk of land, so it all evened out. By the time we got back onto the highway we were on to begin with no time was lost. We took a right and went a few miles and took a left.

The next thirty miles were an absolute wasteland. Nothing but nothing. There were hills and curves, but no rabbits running across the road, no antelope or coyote. At one point we passed a sign for a gypsum field, that's what they use to make sheetrock.

We pulled over in the middle of this so my oldest brother could take a leak. He peed on the front tire. I had to go too. I peed on the back tire. His friend walked into the sagebrush and squatted. When she came back we stood next to the car and rolled a joint, or tried to, or she tried to. It was windy. She got into the shotgun seat and shut the door. Me and my oldest brother watched her for a while and then turned around to check out the landscape.

The air was dry and hot, but we were nearly a mile above sea level. The wind was coming from a canyon nearly thirty miles away, that was part of the Rockies. It smelt like sagebrush and dust. The emptiness made you feel the opposite of alone. I felt connected. I would have lit a cigarette, but it was too windy. My brother's friend got out of the car. She was sucking on the joint making sure it stayed lit. She sucked the smoke in and handed it to my oldest brother, who sucked the smoke in himself and handed it to me. I did the same.

I didn't question why we were smoking a joint on the side of the highway. I already knew why. Cops. Always the cops. All three of us kept a vigil on the horizon. Looking for cars. Vehicles. There was at least five minutes of road between us and the next ridge. On both sides. We finished the joint and got back inside.

I handed my brother and his friend a cigarette. They both thanked me and we pulled back onto the road. When we were about a mile down a highway patrol car crested the horizon. I watched my brother's friend's knuckles go white. I looked at the speedometer. Sixty-five. My oldest brother lit his cigarette and rolled down the window. I instinctively put my cigarette back in the pack and put the pack in the pouch that was connected to the seat in front of me. I stared straight ahead. My oldest brother's friend stared straight ahead. My oldest brother pretended to look in the glove box. Ten seconds. Five seconds. One second. Then he passed.

Me and my oldest brother waited a second and spun our heads around. The highway patrol kept going. His friend could see it in the rearview. Holy shit that was close. What a fucking buzz kill. Tell me about it.

But it wasn't a buzz kill. We stayed high the whole rest of the way.

We took the sneaky road that completely bypassed Lovell and crept easy through the ass end of Powell.

As we passed the city limits we had to slow down. All three of us rolled our windows down. My oldest brother turned the radio to the college station. He had been trying to get it for miles, but eventually gave up. Now it worked. He turned it up. Everything felt different. This was a college town. I lit a cigarette and memorized everything. I felt so fucking sophisticated.

What do you call it when you take something that is right and replace it with something that is correct? Like using a key instead of picking a lock. Or using a crescent wrench instead of channel locks when tightening a bolt? There must be a word for it. Or a phrase for it. Restructuring? Dedicated nuance? Whatever it is, it happened to me. I restructured my emotional well-being with a dedicated nuance when we drove into town.

The town wasn't much bigger than W, but it was a college town. Everything was larger all the sudden. Smarter. Cooler. Kids with cool hairdos. On skateboards. Smoking cigarettes. I saw somebody with a tattoo. Frisbee in the park. It felt different. It was different. It felt like freedom.

My oldest brother's friend drove down the main drag for my benefit, although I believe she got a thrill out of it too.

There were coffee shops and bike shops, and even a head shop. Both of them pointed out bars that were cool to go to, people that they knew, and why. They both slid down in their seats instinctively to look more relaxed. I did too, a mirror of coolness. I'm sure I had a huge smile on my face and looked just like a child watching a conveyor belt carrying bubble gum, but I felt cool. That was all that mattered.

When we got to the end of the drag we took a left and a left again. We had to backtrack to the street we actually needed to turn on. We took a right on Morning Glory. We drove one block and crossed the intersection. We parked and got out of the car.

My oldest brother was living in a rental house with two roommates. A girl from Greybull who was Mary's best friend, and a boy from Gillette that would become my oldest brother's best friend. They had a band called the Plaid Infidels they told me. The band was hypothetical. Not one of them could play an instrument. They had a name though. That was all that mattered.

We left our stuff in the car and went inside. The house was a ranch house, much like the house in W, but minus the basement. It had a large kitchen with a linoleum floor and three bedrooms. The living room smelled like dog shit because the carpet had absorbed years of cigarettes and bong rips and spilled beer. The walls were slightly greasy and yellow. There was a blue beanbag chair in the corner and somebody had written on the wall, in permanent marker: Make Wove Not Lar.

My brain had trouble processing this new information,

but it didn't matter, my oldest brother went to the kitchen and took three beers from the refrigerator and handed them out. We stood there in the middle of the living room. We cracked open the beers. My oldest brother made a toast:

"To Killing The Math!" He held up his beer.

"To Killing The Math!" We all drank as much beer as we could. I got about halfway down before I couldn't drink anymore. I asked him what he meant by that.

"Right brain, left brain. I took a class about it, turns out if you drink enough your right brain turns off, that's where your logic is apparently."

"Who needs logic?" his friend said and chugged the rest of her beer.

"I love logic." I said it without thinking.

"Yeah, mom told me you were doing Chuck's homework for him."

"He's better at other stuff. Dude's gonna take state this year."

"Yeah, but you shouldn't do his homework for him."

"Why not? He's having a hard time. It's been different since you left."

"Yeah, but, so?"

"He just needs help, I want to help him."

"C'mon you two, this is too serious, let's drink another beer!"

My oldest brother's friend was right. This was too serious. It was summer. And we were talking about high school. And my older brother Chuck was going to be a senior next year anyway. Whatever he was up to was his own business. I chugged the rest of my beer. My oldest brother did too. We got new beers. Before long we were half drunk and hoping for action.

Before long we got what we hoped for.

༽༅༅༼

We were standing in the kitchen when somebody yelled through the screen door. It was my oldest brother's soon to be new best friend. He yelled:

"Boat boat boa!" and asked if we could help him out.

He was carrying three cases of beer. My oldest brother's friend ran to the door and opened it for him. My oldest brother took the three cases from his arms and put it on the counter. He introduced me. His name was Michael. He said hi, but he didn't shake my hand. The beer needed to be put in the fridge. Something was about to happen.

It took all of ten minutes before people started showing up. Most of them had beer. Twelve-packs or eighteen-packs. Michael put music on. People started dancing. It was spastic. A guy showed up with a slingshot shooting condoms at people. A gal came in walking on her hands, balancing a pizza on her feet. Before long the house was cramped. I was in love with it when I felt a tug on the sleeve of my shirt.

Mary told me I should take a walk with her. I said ok and followed her out to the side of the house. She pushed me against it and kissed me. I kissed back. She grabbed my dick, which was now hard, through my jeans. Or on top of my jeans. I probably came, or didn't, it didn't matter, I came in my mind. We kissed for a while and then went back inside.

The earth was swimming. I was the deep end.

The hours disappeared like burnt toast, meaning you could scrape their surfaces into the trash and still had something to wipe your knife on. Something better than a pant leg.

I woke up on the beanbag chair with a thirst for water. I was still completely dressed. Wearing shoes. I went into the kitchen and found a glass on the counter by the sink. I rinsed it out and filled it. I drank the water. I did this twice. When I went back into the living room I saw Mary was asleep on the couch. She was using a jacket as a blanket. She was completely dressed as well, except she had taken off her shoes. I wanted to wake her up and see if she wanted to make out some more. I didn't. I sat down on the beanbag chair and went back to sleep.

When I woke up the second time the house was as busy as a dishwasher's hands inside a sack of potatoes. I felt bad I wasn't helping as my oldest brother and Michael cleaned up the wreck from the previous night. There was nothing I could do.

Everybody was hungover. They were too young to see it on their faces, but their movements were sluggish and their eyes were all bright red. I was fine though. I was too excited to be hungover, I sat there in that beanbag waiting for more.

Somebody started the pipe and they all sat down. We passed it around until my eyes became red as well. Nobody said anything until somebody said we should go to Grandma's and get some biscuits and gravy. We left the house and got into Mary's car.

We didn't need to drive to Grandma's but we did. They had a parking lot. We parked and went inside. We sat down in a booth. A waitress came over. We all ordered coffee and a full plate of biscuits with gravy. She was holding a pot of coffee. The cups were upside down on doilies. We flipped them over. Nobody had looked at a menu, so there was no reason to return them to the slot behind the sugar and salt and pepper. They were already there. After she poured the coffee somebody said thanks, it was probably me, my oldest brother and his two friends were out of normal sorts. I poured an imprudent amount of sugar in my coffee and some milk. Somebody said:

"They got the best biscuits and gravy in town. You're in for a treat."

"I'm ok with that." I was too young still to know what to say sometimes.

"First time in Powell?" it was Michael

"Nah, was here with the swim team back in January."

"No shit! I used to dive." His eyes were bright red and bulging. He had long dark hair and a mercurial smile. He looked like a cute hunk. I cute undecided hunk.

"Mary told me, you're a Camel, we kicked your ass at state!"

"Fuck that! Off year, not only that, but we got you guys with both the two hundred fly and the I.M."

"Yeah, but it was your home town! I'd be embarrassed if I was you."

This swimmer talk created an instant bond between us. He smiled like a moped, swift and useful. My oldest brother was sitting next to him drinking his coffee slowly, not saying anything. Mary was sitting next to me pushing her leg against mine and not saying anything as well. I was hard again. I was so hard in fact that I was nearly creaming my jeans.

The biscuits with gravy arrived. I watched my oldest brother and his friends put salt and pepper and hot sauce on top. I did the same. They were tasty and spicy. I scraped my fork against the plate until there was nothing left. Had I been alone I would have used my finger to wipe up the final residue. But I wasn't.

We paid and went back to the car. Nobody said anything on the way back to the house. When we got there my oldest brother and Michael went back to bed.

Me and Mary sat on the couch. She turned on the television. She slid over to me on the couch. Before I knew it we were making out and she had my dick in her hand. I came so hard it socked me in the jaw and nearly knocked me out. It took me all of two seconds to recover. The air was explosive with butterfly wings. I could hear their silent flapping. Gossamer.

Mary fell asleep. The jacket she had used as a blanket had fallen to the floor. I picked it up and draped it over her shoulders. She wasn't wearing socks. I decided her feet were cold. I took the beanbag I was sleeping on a put it on her legs. She looked peaceful lying there on the couch. I decided to go for a walk.

I had no idea where I was going, and I didn't really know where I was, so I took a left and tried to recreate the drive into town, that way I could at least get back. I noted the house number before I left, 3006, like the bullet, and went walking.

It was strange the way Powell resembled W, some of the houses were exactly the same as the ones in W, and although it was closer to the mountains, the town was still in the Big Horn Basin, which meant it was at Wyoming sea level, which was five thousand feet.

I got to the main drag and decided to stop. There was nothing to do but light a cigarette. I lit a cigarette and decided to do nothing.

The main drag was a wonderful scary place. A guy walked by me holding a sign that said: Your Heart Is A Balloon-Don't Fill It With Hate-It Will Pop. There was a girl using a lampshade as an umbrella, she had taped it to a tree branch.

I stood there long enough to realize I should keep walking. The rest of the main drag was more of the same. People must have known that I smoked, because I had bummed out half my pack of cigarettes by the time I made it to the train tracks that split the good part of town from the bad part of town. I crossed the tracks and it was no longer jovial. I walked a couple more blocks and got bored of the surroundings. It was just houses and traffic. I could see that the road I was on just led to more housing on one side, and fields of corn on the left. I turned around.

When I got back to my oldest brother's house I still had most of the cigarettes I had left after bumming half of them out. I took the street parallel to the main drag to avoid the bums. The street was quiet. I walked in without knocking.

My oldest brother was awake now, he was standing in the kitchen with Michael and Mary. He said hi and asked me where I had been. He handed me a beer. They were all drinking beer. They didn't look hungover any longer. I told them about the walk and asked about what was going to happen tonight. My oldest brother said:

"I'd say, not nothing, I got to work tomorrow." Michael nodded. They worked together.

"Yeah, and I gotta haul ass back to Greybull and feed them damn dogs, you are more than welcome to come with me, I can get you to W whenever." Mary said this in a way that made my oldest brother realize there was some hanky-panky happening. He understood it was an invitation to me that meant more than what was said. He pursed his lips and smiled out of the corner of his mouth.

"You should do that," he said.

"Yeah, ok."

I was excited about this idea. I tried my best to hide my excitement. We drank the beers and my oldest brother followed us to Mary's car to grab his shit. We said goodbye to him and got in the car. He told me to call mom as we drove away. I said I would. He smiled and shook his head.

The ride out of town was awkward. I personally had nothing to say. I had also been so turned on that my dick hurt and was starting to leak into my jeans. It was hard to hide, but I did my best. She must have known. I was sixteen and she was twenty-one. That's like a lifetime, times two, in teenage years, by difference in age . Had she touched me I probably would have exploded and died. She didn't though. The conversation was menial. We listened to the radio. I lit her cigarettes.

When we got to the road where we could take a right and bypass town we took a left. We passed a grove of cottonwood trees that was too beautiful to describe, and a graveyard of old airplanes, we crossed a the Bighorn River and dropped into town. The speed limit dropped from sixty-five to forty-five to thirty. We passed the new high school and the two gas stations. We went through the drive-through at the liquor store and got a twelve-pack. The underage laws didn't apply in this county. She handed it to me. I put it on the floor between my feet. We turned around and went back to the school and took a right by the grocery store. When we got to the edge of the town, where the hills met the town, we pulled into the driveway.

She got out and went immediately to the side of the house. I got out and put the beer on top of the car and followed her. She was playing with the dogs over the fence. Saying nice things to them. Telling them she missed them. And sorry. Sorry she was away for so long.

She grabbed a big bag of dog food from the garage and took it into the fenced off area. She filled their bowls. She took a hose from the side of the house and filled their water bowls. One was a Husky, the other a Labrador. They were wagging their tails so hard I was afraid they would flip over and roll around on the ground like wind-up toys. They didn't. They instead ate the food and ran around biting each other's legs.

Mary's house was in a pocket. It felt like a pocket. There was something about its location that seemed crowded. Shoved, even. It was next to a cliff, quite literally on the edge of town.

It was a ranch house, and it had no basement. The kitchen had a sliding glass door that led to the backyard. The backyard led to the cliff. There was a cottonwood tree with a swing made from a tire. The grass was lumpy.

The house itself had three bedrooms and a living room where my Mary's mother died from cancer on a gurney. The driveway was large enough for two cars. There was a house across the street, but it was down and over. Aside from this the house was essentially a burp. A release from town.

When Mary finished feeding the dogs she took me inside. The house smelled of lavender and there was a hallway that led to the bathroom. Her bedroom was just left of the front door. We went inside and sat down on the bed, next to each other. Her father wasn't home, he had a girlfriend, she said. Her sister lived in Nevada just outside of Reno. Her other sister lived in Billings. We didn't shut the door.

There was no talking. Our silence turned into kissing.

Our kissing turned into groping. Our groping turned into a handjob. The handjob turned into a blowjob. The blowjob made me come in her mouth. I went cross-eyed for a moment as she spit the come on my stomach. I was confused. I didn't know it was possible to feel this good.

She used her sheets to wipe the come from my stomach. Her sheets were blue. I said thanks. She smiled. My dick shrunk from gorging to flaccid. I pulled my pants up. I followed her into the kitchen.

There was liquor on the counter. She decided to make us a cocktail. As she was getting ice from the freezer I went out to the car and got the beer. When I got back to the kitchen I put the beer on the counter. She handed me a gin and tonic. I said thanks and took a drink. It was bitter. The glass tasted like lime.

We went outside and sat on a couple of rusty chairs that were in the shade of the house. There was nothing to look at except the cliff and the tree with its tire swing, the dogs and the lumpy lawn. As much as I hated the beauty of Wyoming, I found the absence of it claustrophobic. But I also didn't care. I was sitting on a rusty chair in the backyard of a friend of my oldest brother's drinking a gin and tonic. Not only that, but I had just been given an amazing blowjob. Not only that, but I was away from my hometown and my stupid job and my jerk friends. Not only that, but I was sitting on a rusty chair drinking a gin and tonic with a girl that just gave me a blowjob. I was sitting on top of the fucking world.

After an hour of sitting on rusty chairs drinking gin and tonics Mary got a little bored. Or uncomfortable. We didn't have much to talk about. She decided to call her friend that lived across the street. She was back from college as well, and was living with her parents for the summer. She came right over. She joined us, sitting down on the lumpy grass and we drank beer instead of gin and tonics. She helped us smoke our cigarettes. Her name was Shannon and she was kind of frumpy with dark brown hair. There was something about her that was very un-sexual. She seemed quite intelligent and deeply angry. I never did figure out why she was so angry. Her life was as simple as ours, and even more so. Her parents were still together. Her brother had moved out of the house and was living with some woman he had knocked up in Basin. My guess was that it was hard to be smart and frumpy and a woman in Wyoming.

I was angry too, but not because I was smart and frumpy. I got sick of being picked on by idiot cowboys with nothing better to do than chase me around in their pickup trucks. Of being told to get a job, because that is what you do. I was angry that I needed to be part of the failing system if I was to survive. I wanted more, but as far as I could tell, there was nothing more to be had. I was frustrated because I wanted out. I was frustrated and it made me angry.

We drank beer and listened to classic rock on the radio. Eventually the sun went down. A street light went on that made the light grainy and brought out the nighthawks. Mary and her friend from across the street did cartwheels and handstands in the lumpy grass. The dogs did some barking and the night ended when the moon came up over the cliff. Shannon needed to hit the sack. She had to work in the morning. Mary did too. They worked at the same place, as waitresses, at a café called Marie's. They had the morning shift. We decided to go swimming the next day when they were finished. I must have been drunk because I don't remember going to bed or anything that happened afterwards, but I do remember waking up in the morning.

❧

My oldest brother's friend was gone. I was greatly relieved. I hadn't taken a shit in two days, and being around two girls the night before made it an impossible embarrassment. I don't think I have ever felt so empty afterwards.

I went out to the car to get my bag, but it was gone. I went back in and found it on the couch with a note that said there was food and coffee if I wanted. I dug in my bag. I took out my toothbrush and a clean pair of boxers. I took a shower. I brushed my teeth. I put on clean underwear.

In the kitchen I found the coffee she was talking about. I poured a cup and looked for the food she meant. It wasn't obvious. I ended up toasting a piece of bread and putting peanut butter on it. It was quite tasty. I made another. I ate it and finished my coffee. I didn't know what to do with myself. I looked around the house for a while, but then felt weird, like her dad would show up at any moment, although he was out of town Mary told me he might show up at any moment. I decided to go buy more cigarettes.

When I got back to house her father's car was in the driveway. I decided to keep walking. I walked back around the house via a route that kept me hidden from view. I had to scramble up a vertical cliff. The dirt broke off as climbed and I was sweaty and dusty when I got to the top. I sat down and looked at house. I lit a cigarette and watched her father feed the dogs. He was a short, swarthy man, with Native American features. Quite handsome, in fact. He had a short military haircut. He was very nice to the dogs. They were happy to see him. I stood up and went walking.

❧

There was nothing but badlands in front of me. Badlands that ended at the mountains. After a while I turned around to see where I came from. The town was no longer available to look at. The sun was already hot, and the grasshoppers sounded like rattle snakes. I got sick of worrying I would get bit and turned around. I got to the cliff and scrambled back to the bottom. The dogs barked at me, but her father didn't come out. I went around the front and saw his car was no longer there. I didn't go inside. There was no point to risk it. I kept walking.

I made it to the turn of the road that went up Shell Canyon and took a left. I stopped in front of Marie's and saw Mary and Shannon working the lunch shift. They were busy. The place was crowded. I thought about going inside, but I didn't. I walked over to the main street and found a newspaper box. I bought a copy of the Northern Wyoming Daily News. I pushed the button and my quarter came back out. I put it in my pocket. I sat down in front of a store that had a bench out front. It sold western clothes. Cowboy boots and brush poppers. There was a bank across the street that had a sign which would tell you the time and the temperature. It was 12:13 P.M. 95 degrees Fahrenheit.

I was sitting in the shade.

It took an hour before I was so bored that I could puke. I threw the paper away and walked down the street. I went into the gas station where I bought the cigarettes and found the microwave burritos. I went for the chicken chimichanga. I sat on one of the parking curbs as I ate the burrito. When I was done I went to the pay phone and dialed 1-800-HOT-BOYS. The answering service told me how to get in touch with the hot boys. I laughed. I still had another hour to burn. I could tell because I could see the bank sign. I craved action, but there was nothing I could do about it.

The hour burned like a snail's broken heart. Indifferent to perspective. The sun beat down like salt. It left a grease stain that was of the opposite of motion. Screaming in silence. Immobile.

I was so bored I nearly puked. At one point I stood up and kicked my legs hoping to stimulate something other than my mind. Somebody was going into the gas station as I did this. They gave me a weird look. I said go fuck yourself. They looked horrified and hurried inside. I looked through the window and could see the guy talking to the cashier about me. The cashier looked out the window shaking his head. He was wearing a red smock. I flipped him the bird and walked towards the school that was next to the gas station. I thought for sure he would come out and yell at me, but he didn't. Good for him, I thought, fucking loser.

I walked along the main road toward the bridge leading into town. My body felt like a snake being held in the middle trying to break loose, and my mind felt like a flamboyant baboon. Had I not been where I was, I would have been elsewhere for sure. Anywhere I guess. Just not here. But I don't think that that wouldn't have even mattered.

I went under the bridge to get out of the heat. The

river was brown and infuriating. I couldn't come to terms about how pissed off I was, that I was so angry. I snuck into the tall grass along the edge of the bridge and laid down and masturbated. I felt a little less angry. I listened to cars and trucks drive over the bridge. I would have fallen asleep, but there were too many bugs and grasshoppers. I didn't know how to deal with the come on my stomach, so I ignored it. I stood up and fastened my jeans. The come turned to liquid and ran down my leg. This made me feel weird, so I took everything out of my pockets and put it on the ground. I took my shoes and socks off, and my shirt. I waded into the water. Halfway into the river I was still only thigh-deep. I bent down and grabbed some grass that was on the bottom. I held the grass and let the current try to pull my body away. After a moment I let go. I floated into the sunlight. My eyes were closed. I had a brief moment of peace before I panicked and stood up. I cut my feet on rocks as I pushed against the current to get back to my stuff.

When I got back to my stuff my feet were too muddy to put into my socks and my jeans were too wet to be useful. I wadded everything up into my shirt. I walked back up and around the bridge and onto the road. A truck came by just at that moment and the kid sitting shotgun threw a can at me. Fucking hippy, he yelled.

I stood on the side of the road long enough for my feet to dry. They were still dirty when I put them into my socks, but I didn't care anymore. I put my shirt back on and then my shoes. All the things that were in my pocket didn't really matter if they got wet, so I shoved them back in. The only things that mattered were my smokes and my lighter. I held them in my hand as I walked back toward town.

When I got back to Mary's house I sat down on the slab of concrete that made up her front doorstep. I lit a cigarette.

I took my shoes off and my socks. I took the things back out of my pockets and laid them out to dry. Everything smelled like dirt. I, personally, smelled like a ditch.

꙳

I sat there drying out for quite some time. I felt like a worm that had squirmed out from the earth during a rainstorm, that had wriggled onto the sidewalk to breathe. It was hot and dry and I was helpless and stuck. Luckily I wasn't a worm though, so I scooted into the shade.

Thirty minutes went by before Mary and Shannon showed back up. I was counting ants when they pulled into the driveway. There was no fanfare and Mary went inside as me and her friend made small talk.

We really didn't have anything to talk about. I mean, she was five years older than me, and could drink legally, and I was just some kid that was the brother of a friend of theirs. But she tried, and I tried. And there was lots and lots of silence.

During the silence we learned the reason Mary went inside. And it was an unbelievable amount of noise that came out the bathroom window from around the side of the house. The window was left open. From before. Shannon and I went from being awkward to terrifyingly awkward. I lit a cigarette because of it and tried to talk louder. It didn't help.

A few minutes later Mary came outside holding two women's bathing suits. She told us she was Douglass. It turned out that in her family they called taking a shit taking a Doug, and when you were done you were Douglass. Her friend turned bright red. I smiled.

We got in the car and backed out of the driveway. I was sitting in the back. As we were driving away, Mary said oh shit and slammed on the brakes and took the car out of first and put it in neutral and pulled the emergency brake. She left the door open as she ran inside. The radio was on. When she came back she was holding a bottle of whiskey. She handed it to me through the open window and got back inside. She slammed the door and sped off.

It took twenty minutes to get to the pond that was the best place to swim. When we parked they changed into their swimming suits. I pretended not to watch them undress, but I couldn't. Their bushes glistening in the late afternoon sun. And their breasts. I kicked a rock and tried not to explode.

All I had to do to get ready to swim was to kick off my shoes and take off my socks and shirt, and remove my jeans. I was wearing boxers.

When they were finished changing my boner luckily was gone and somebody asked if we were ready. We all ran into the water. The ground was nothing but mud and reeds. It was a little unpleasant, but when we were waist-deep we all dove in. The water was warm and turned brown because we stirred up so much of the bottom. When Mary came up for air she had a large amount of snot coming out of her nose. I didn't know how to tell her about it, so I dove back into the water hoping it would be gone when I came back up. It was, but I don't know why it was gone. Maybe her friend told her about it, or maybe she just naturally wiped her nose. We frolicked for a while. It was hard not to look at their breasts. Their swimming suits were flimsy.

I couldn't take it any more so I waded back to shore.

I sat on the hood of the car and dried off. I watched them swim. Some ducks landed on the pond and stuck their heads in the water. I wanted to drink some of the whiskey, but I felt like I wasn't allowed to. Eventually they walked up onto the shore, muddy and smiling.

Their bathing suits dripping from their bodies. Nipples taut. Their pubic hair was the only thing holding up the bottoms. It nearly killed me.

I pretended to look at a bird as they walked to the car. The sun burned my eyes and I was glad for it. I was seeing spots as they got dressed again.

After they were dressed Mary turned the car on. She wanted to play the radio without the battery dying out. She found the whiskey and joined me sitting on the hood of the car. She took a swig from the bottle and handed it me. I took a swig myself and handed it her friend. I decided to get dressed myself. All four doors were open so we could hear the music. Even the hatch on the back. I got dressed and walked around to the front of the car and stood there trying to look cool. I lit a cigarette and they told me the disc jockey was a friend of theirs, a certain Shane that was in a local band called Caution Tape. He was playing country music, but it was ironic country music. On the radio. And his band had a local celebrity status that even I had heard of. They told me his girlfriend was a friend of theirs and we should go hang out with them later tonight. They had a farm on the hill up past the senior center on the way out of town. I thought this was an excellent idea.

The bottle of whiskey got passed around again. A huge gust of wind came and blew a cloud of dust in our eyes. All the packs of cigarettes went flying and the bottle of whiskey that was sitting on the hood tipped over. It was square though, so it didn't roll onto the ground. And the lid was tightened. I picked up the cigarettes and we gathered our things to leave. A thunderstorm was blowing in.

Huge drops of dirt-filled raindrops started hitting the car as we pulled back onto the highway. This was lucky. We could have easily been stuck on the dirt road. The Tercel had four-wheel drive, but it also had street tires, and it hadn't rained in at least a week, so the road could have turned into slick mud in a matter of seconds. As it was though, the highway wasn't much better. We fishtailed as we pulled onto the pavement. Freshly wet asphalt is the most slippery. The sky was almost black with clouds and the rain sounded like golf balls hitting the roof. The rain turned to hail for a minute, and then back to rain again. The windshield wipers were going full blast, but we couldn't see shit. Mary turned on headlights and crept along the highway at about twenty miles an hour keeping her eye in the rearview just in case someone was about to come barreling upon us from behind. Lightning lit up the sky in spastic volts, and the register of the thunder shook the car. It was terribly exciting. The radio had been turned of immediately because of the storm. In between the thunder was silence.

Just like that though, the storm passed. The sky cleared and the sun beat down like a hysterical scream from the sky. We all rolled our windows down. The smell of fresh earth and sagebrush came rushing in. The sound of the rain-drenched asphalt throwing water into the wheel wells as the tires themselves grasped desperately for traction. It was always a moment of peace just after a storm. Every single time. Then came the sound of the birds, you could even see them, flying from brush to brush. Then of course a rainbow. And just like that, back to normal.

The radio went back on. We all lit cigarettes. We even passed the bottle of whiskey around, although I personally only drank a tiny drink. Hard liquor. Hard to swallow.

When we got back to Mary's house it looked like

a tornado had come through town. The trees were all intact, but the house was covered in debris. Leaves were stuck to everything. A green tarp that had been left in the backyard was dangling from a fence. A garden gnome that I hadn't noticed before was tipped over. There was a huge puddle on the corner where a sidewalk should be. The screen door was open and bent a little. We pulled into the driveway and got out.

Me and Mary went to get the tarp. Her friend went inside to make sandwiches. I couldn't remember eating anything. So this was nice of her. Mary and I took the tarp to the backyard and stretched it out to dry. She went to check on the dogs. I went inside.

I went to the bathroom and looked out the window as I took a leak. I could see Mary petting the dogs and feeding them. I flushed and went into the kitchen. Her friend had three plates on the counter and was spreading salad dressing on white bread. There was a stack of American cheese and head of iceberg lettuce. There was also a stack of beef baloney and a bag of potato chips.

When Mary came in she said:

"Man! Those poor dogs, wet as the day is, what you makin' there, Bo-log-na? What we drinkin'?"

There wasn't any more talk. Mary made three drinks and her friend made three sandwiches with chips. I stood there unhelpful. After a while we were outside on the back porch sitting down, eating baloney sandwiches with chips and drinking gin with tonic and ice, not talking to each other and looking at a cliff and a tree, watching the shadows of the sunset push itself upon us.

꒰꒱

The shadow play acted out its own death, feeling no more. The phone rang. The silence was broken. Mary ran into the house to answer it. She tripped on the threshold stubbing her toe on the track of the screen door. She said god damn it! And answered the phone:

"Hello," then silence. Her friend and I were listening intently. "Ok, I don't know, an hour?" Then silence. Then she hung up the phone. She came back outside. "That was Winterlude. We should go out there."

"Oh great, did she know we were thinking of coming anyway?" Shannon.

"Don't know, didn't ask."

We reverted to silence and finished our drinks. Mary made another round. She turned the stereo on before coming back out. The evening became exciting. We drank the drinks this time faster than the last ones. Soon we were all back inside acting giddy. A few dance moves were performed. I was put in charge of making more drinks as the girls got ready. I didn't know what I was doing, and I was too embarrassed to ask.

I stood at the counter looking at three empty glasses and the bottle of gin and the bottle of tonic deciding how to proceed. I could hear the girls running back and forth between the bathroom and Mary's bedroom. They were putting on clothes and taking them off. And makeup. Every now and then there was a, "How's this?" followed by a "Looks great!" I gathered all my confidence and opened the bottle of gin. I poured way too much in every glass, filling them nearly half full of gin. I took the ice tray from the freezer, and tried to figure out how it worked. I didn't have ice at home, and if I did it came from a bag that was in the chest freezer on the back porch. I was about to bang it against the counter when I noticed it was flexible and the ice cracked a little when I bent it. I bent the ice cubes out of their frozen cubbies.

I thought maybe I should use a spoon to remove them but instead just dumped them on the counter. I filled each glass to the top. The remaining cubes I put back into the tray and put it back in the freezer. The counter was now wet. I didn't know what to do about this so I looked around. There was a dishrag wadded and wet in the kitchen sink. I wiped it on the counter making matters worse. Now everything was wet and smelled like mildew. I don't know why it didn't occur to me to wring it out. I put the rag back in the sink. I filled the glasses to the top with tonic water.

I took two glasses to the living room and handed them to the girls. They both took a sip and said Jesus Christ! And made eyes like balloons. I shrugged my shoulders and went back into the kitchen partially defeated. There was still the matter of the wet countertop. I took a drink of my own glass and immediately understood their revulsion. The drink was nothing but gin and smelled like mildew. A minute later Mary came in and took a dry towel from a kitchen drawer and wiped the counter down. She took a spoon from another drawer and stirred my drink. She took the spoon with her back to her room.

I took my drink outside onto the back porch and took a drink. It tasted better. I lit a cigarette and waited. I wasn't used to girls getting ready to do things. I wanted to watch but I knew it was imprecate . I listened as they yelled at each other from across the house to each other. Smoking my cigarette. Drinking the gin with a splash of tonic.

Twenty minutes went by before they were ready. But they weren't ready yet. They came out to the back porch wearing skirts and flimsy shirts. They had makeup on and their hair was at weird angles. It was attractive and confusing. I didn't even brush my teeth, but I felt like it was somehow too late to do that now. They both lit cigarettes and talked like we were about to meet the queen of Sweden:

"Should we get a bottle of wine?"

"I don't know, they gotta have liquor, but we can't show up empty handed."

"We should get some smokes."

"And a loaf of bread."

I couldn't enter this conversation, so I just drank my drink as fast as I could, which wasn't fast. The drink was too strong. They finished theirs in minutes and said we should go. Mary took my drink out of my hand and slammed the rest of it. I shrugged my shoulders feeling grateful. We cleaned up the table and put the glasses in the sink. The music was done playing and Mary turned off all the lights. And the stereo. We went outside and got in her car.

As we drove through town we pulled into the drive through of the liquor store. We got a bottle of white wine and three packs of cigarettes. We drove up over the viaduct and down into the river valley and up the hill. We took a right on a dirt road just south of town. We passed a large shed and a pasture. We came to a house that had all its lights on. Music was blaring out. The house was rustic, meaning dilapidated. It was made of wood. It looked like a cabin almost, except it was a house. The driveway was just a dirt lot.

The house was on a cliff. The cliff looked over the town. The moon was just now coming over the hills to the west of us. A dog barked in the distance. The sound of horses snorting. Making hoof noises on the ground. And the sound of music coming from inside.

We parked the car and got out. We walked silently to the front door. Carrying our bottle of wine and three packs of cigarettes. We didn't get bread. Somebody knocked on the door. The door opened. A tall man with long brown hair opened it. He said, oh shit! Mare Bear! Shanty! Welcome to Chez le roux! And who is this fine hunk of meat?

I shook his hand and somebody told him my name and my story. We went inside.

The house had a mudroom. The mudroom had a horse blanket flap. The tall man pulled it to the side so we could walk in.

The house was indeed a cabin. A large cabin with a balcony, living room and an anteroom. The living room contained the kitchen. Or the things that make up a kitchen. A sink. A counter. A refrigerator. Their friend was in the kitchen smoking a cigarette by the window. She looked at us and said, "look what the cat dragged in."

Mary handed her the wine and the cigarettes and said, we've come bearing gifts. I became introduced, and we all settled in, to what seemed to me at the time, some serious drinking.

After half an hour the bottle of wine was gone and half a pack of cigarettes. They were nice to me and knew my oldest brother. We talked about music and I played them two songs I had been working on. This surprised Mary, she didn't know I could play guitar, but in the end the songs just embarrassed everyone except the tall man, Shane, who took the guitar from me and proceeded to play covers of classic rock tunes.

We eventually ended up in the anteroom sitting on the couch drinking beer. Shane sat in a chair by the window and Winterlude sat on the floor. Their friend was wearing a long cotton flowered dress, and when she sat down she pulled it up over her knees and sat Indian style. She wasn't wearing any panties. And as her boyfriend told us a story about her mother coming over it took all my effort to not to stare at her hairy crotch.

"So you know, I don't know, I was full of morning glory," meaning hard on, "and we were just waking up, and Winty here is pushing her ass against me, so you know, whatever, and halfway through her mom comes barreling into the house yacking about how half the hay fell out the back of the truck, and I'm trying to hold my shit in, but shit, she laughs and fucking sure as shit, I blow my load while her mom is standing there!"

We all laughed and I took the opportunity to look at their friends hairy crotch. Luckily she stood up soon after to get us more beer and saved me from my misery. I could have cried I was so acutely aware of it.

The rest of the night went nowhere. We ended up stupid and handsome, stumbling to the car. There was the normal, are you ok to drive followed by the requisite, of course. The drive back through town was luckily uneventful.

When we got back to Mary's house we went inside and all hopped in the same bed. Nothing happened sadly and we all fell asleep.

In the morning Mary's alarm went off. She had to go to work. Her friend however didn't. Both of us lay in bed trying to sleep as she got ready for work. The front door slammed and you could hear it as she started the car and pulled out of the driveway. Then there was silence again.

Apparently she and her friend had made an arrangement that I was unaware of, because after she drove away she cuddled up to me and put her hand on my dick and said:

"She and I made an arrangement."

I didn't mind. I turned over and kissed her. There was almost nothing sexual about it. She gave me a very lazy hand job and went back to sleep. Where I was exited before I was now just confused. I tried to go back to sleep but I couldn't. I got up and went into the kitchen to make some coffee.

I stood in the kitchen feeling something I had never felt before, violated. I mean I was ok with it, but I didn't understand why nobody had never told me about this before. I found myself in some interim state, poised in statue, watching the world unfold in front of me. I wanted to scream but I couldn't. I was frozen.

I made some coffee because that was something I knew how to do. I was hungry and ate a piece of cheese. When the coffee was finished brewing I poured two cups and took them both into Mary's bedroom. I put one on the nightstand and woke her friend up. I asked her if she wanted it. She said yeah maybe and went back to sleep. I took my cup of coffee and went out on the back porch. I sat down and lit a cigarette. The backyard was shady, but it was already hot. I kind of wanted to leave, but I really wanted to stay. I remembered the check I had that was supposed to be left for me back home. I called my house. My youngest brother answered:

"Hello?"

"Hey puke, is mom there?"

"She's at the storage units."

"Shit, it's Tuesday. Do you know if Kenny left a check for me?"

"I don't know. Where are you?"

"In Greybull. Can you look around?" He put the phone down.

"I don't see it."

"Fuck. Ok. How's your butt?"

"Full of poop, how's yours?"

"Ha! Same. Can you tell her to deposit it for me if it came?"

"Ok. When are you coming home?"

"I don't know, soon."

"Ok."

"Ok."

I hung up the phone. I missed my brother. I felt an ache. I decided to take a shower.

The shower was terrible. I didn't know the knobs. I turned on the hot water thinking it was the cold water. I undressed and stood in the tub. I pulled the parasol. I expected a cold shock. I instead was doused in what felt like hot lava. I slipped and fell into the tub. I let out a shriek. I scrambled naked over the edge of the tub. I laid there catching my breath. Are you ok? Came from beyond the door. I'm fine, I yelled as I stood up. I adjusted the water and went to get back in when I caught a glimpse of myself in the mirror. My body was bright red.

The rest of the shower was ok enough. I can't say I enjoyed it though.

When I finished I dried off with a towel that smelt of mildew and I put my clothes back on. I brushed my teeth and went into the living room.

I turned the radio on. The sound music was immediately followed by:

"What the hell! Turn that shit off! I'm trying to sleep!" coming from the bedroom.

"It's ten in the morning Shannon!"

"So fucking what!" I didn't turn the radio off. I did the opposite. I turned it up.

"Fucking Christ!" She came storming out of the bedroom, her huge breasts naked and frumpy. Her bush, like an Italian order of black curly fries. I wasn't being insolent on purpose, but I was a little pissed at being taken advantage of.

"What ya gonna do?" I stepped back. I couldn't help it but my dick was as hard as a day old plucked goose. She pushed the power button. She turned around and went back into the bedroom. I thought about turning the radio back on, but instead I went back into the bathroom and locked the door. I laid down on the floor and unbuttoned my pants. I masturbated to the thought of her naked ass walking away from me after the argument. Afterwards I felt ashamed. I could have punched something. I instead cleaned myself up with some toilet paper and put it in the toilet and flushed.

What the fuck? Was my only thought as I stormed out the front door. I chased a cat out of the lawn and made my way into town. I lit a smoke and barked back at a dog that was barking at me from behind a chain link fence. I could smell the hay harvest from the south side of town blowing through my nostrils. There was the sound of a train coming through town on its way to W to pick up the early wheat harvest, it made me angry. It made me angry that I knew this.

I walked by Marie's and looked inside. The morning rush. I should have gone inside and had breakfast. I saw Mary working her ass off. It was too much so I kept walking.

I crossed the river bridge that led up Shell Canyon. I didn't know where I was going, but I didn't care, as long as it was out of town. I walked along the highway on the left side, against the traffic paying attention to the license plates of the tourists coming in from the canyon. I counted three from Nevada and one from California.

The rest were mostly Niners. This being county nine. Big Horn.

I got hot and decided to climb up the hill next to the highway and find some shade. I found a cliff and sat down. A rattlesnake that I hadn't seen shook its tail. I jumped away without thinking. This was a bad maneuver. When alarmed they strike. I was apparently stealing its shade. I scrambled up and around the cliff and took refuge under an aspen tree. I was glad I hadn't been bitten and the shock cleared my mind. I was hungry and I should probably eat something.

I made my way back to the highway avoiding the cliff with the rattlesnake. I slipped and scraped my elbow. The dirt was so dry that it could draw moisture from salt. I looked at the blood coming from my elbow only out of reflex. It didn't register. It was already scabbing.

When I got to Marie's I walked inside. The door had a bell that rang. The morning rush was gone. I stood by the sign that told me to wait to be seated. I waited to be seated. There was nobody inside the café except for a couple looking at a map. And the staff.

Eventually Mary saw me and came over. She said:

"Hi, where's Shannon?"

"I don't know, sleeping."

"Here to eat?"

"I'm hungry, you on break?"

"Not yet, come with me."

She led me to a table and asked me if I wanted coffee. I did. She handed me a menu. She went into the kitchen. When she came back she put a cup of coffee in front of me, she said:

"That was fun last night, those two are a trip, right? Why didn't Shanny come with you?"

"I don't know, think she's hung over, she barked at me for turning on the stereo."

"She likes her silence. Want something?"

"Biscuits and gravy."

"Eggs?"

"Nah."

"Give me a sec, I'll come hang out, gotta roll some silverware."

She went back to the kitchen. A couple minutes later she came back with a plate and put it down in front of me. She went over to the counter and grabbed a grey bin with four partitioned troughs. She put it on the table. One of the troughs had forks, one spoons, one knifes. The other had napkins and brown paper wraparounds that had a sticky end. She started talking:

"She give you the goose?" I had put salt and pepper on the biscuits with gravy, and hot sauce. I was drinking my coffee black.

"Yeah, what the hell was that about?"

"I thought you would like it, her too."

"Yeah, but, she really doesn't like me. I feel awkward."

"Eh, it will be fine." She didn't take her eyes off the silverware. She was very fast.

"Yeah, well."

"Yeah, well, we can talk about it later." She had a stack of rolled silverware in the trough where the napkins had started. Her lack of emotion made me want to fuck her. I was finished with my breakfast so I stood up and went into the bathroom. I masturbated to the thought of her bending over the table. I wanted to reach into my balls and pull out everything that made me feel this way and be done with it forever. I cleaned up and washed my hands.

When I got back she was no longer at the table. I found her smoking on the street. She smelled like sweaty lipstick . I told her I didn't have any money. She told me not to worry about it. She would be back at the house after the lunch rush. I said thanks and lit a cigarette myself. I heard the bell from the door ring when I got to the corner.

꤮

When I got back to Mary's, Shannon was gone, thank god. I decided to take a nap.

The nap was long and hard, like an antelope's windpipe. I dreamed of death. A terrible car crash from turning too fast around a corner. I found myself as a ghost talking to the M.E. as he autopsied my body. He said I was pretty fucked up. I was impressed with myself for lasting so long in the afterlife. I woke up with a sense of accomplishment.

I was smoking a cigarette on the front porch counting ants and looking at my naked toes when Mary pulled into the driveway. She said, shit, I got to pee, but don't go nowhere, and ran inside. When she came back out she sat down next to me and asked for a drag. I handed her my cigarette. Let's do something, she said and stood back up. I said wait, I gotta get my shoes.

The drive up Shell canyon was slow and terrifying. The highway dropped down into the canyon a thousand feet at least, and there wasn't a single guardrail. I hated it. I hid my nervousness by adjusting the radio. Eventually we no longer got any reception. I couldn't pretend any more. I just looked straight forward with my right eye closed, hoping she wouldn't notice. I chain smoked cigarettes.

When we pulled into the runaway truck pull-off I started to sweat because I was so glad we were stopping. I probably looked like a prime rib being smacked with a slice of Swiss cheese. Holey but mordant. The only thing to hold on to was my sense of humor. Maybe we should chock the wheels? I said. Oh, you are such a pussy, she said slamming her car door and sprinting down the hill.

I didn't catch up to her until she reached the bottom of the canyon. She had taken off her shoes and was wading into the creek. She was wearing cut-off jean shorts and a white t-shirt. I would have fallen in love with her at that moment if that was something I was capable of doing, but instead I took my own shoes off and rolled up my jean legs.

She waded out onto a huge rock that was flat. She laid down and exposed her stomach to the sun. I waded out stumbling like the clumsy jerk that I was, and joined her lying down.

The sun beat down like strips of mercury coming and going as the clouds swept by. The sounds of insects was only ever taken over when more than one boulder decided to move down creek bed at the same time. Had time become something tangible, like a sandwich, I would have swallowed it whole. The air smelled like dandelions and pine. I could have broken the world over my leg like a stick.

We laid there in the sun on that rock until I couldn't take it anymore. We were head to feet. The next thing I remember is touching her leg. Her naked beautiful leg. Her knee. And then her thigh. And then, by all the glory that exists, I slid my hand up her cut-off jeans and past her satin panties, and into her fluid bush.

I didn't really know what to do, so I just kind of rubbed my fingers up and down. She liked it and moaned, but it didn't last long. I realized I was a fool and rolled over into the creek. The water was colder than I thought it would be. I stood up gasping for air. She laughed and told me I was an idiot. I took this as a sign she still liked me and pretended to adjust a tie I wasn't wearing.

I climbed back on the rock and she told me about

how her mom died in her living room and how it fucked her dad up, and how it affected her and her sisters. And once again, I should have fallen in love, but I was too young, and I didn't know how.

Coming down from the canyon was more terrifying than going up. Mary coasted in fourth gear the whole time. She only dropped into third when absolutely necessary. Like when the signs said we should be going twenty-five. I must have looked white because she told me to stop being a wuss. She looked straight ahead and had herself a blast, curving around corners like a hell bat, laughing when the tires screeched. I, however, could look at nothing but the glove box. Catching the road unfold through the tops of my eyes. Eating my cheeks.

When we took the last curve and finally rolled into town I was able to relax. I rolled down the window and lit a cigarette. I handed it to her and lit one for myself. The town was deader than normal. We had to wait for a man pushing a herd of cattle on his horse across the road before we could take the right that led to her house. We weren't inside for more than ten seconds before we were on her bed making out. I know we didn't have sex, because we never had sex. She was worried about sullying me. I didn't know how to tell her I wanted to be soiled. We played around with my dick and she taught me how to eat her out. Afterwards I was thirsty and drank a glass of milk.

The afternoon drifted into the evening and around nine her friend came back over. She sat down with us. Mary and I were sitting on the back porch drinking gin and smoking cigarettes, talking about how come nobody ate Spam anymore. I stood up to get us drinks and Mary said, "no thank you, I'll get it! Your last one was a stinker." We all laughed and she went inside.

When she came back out she handed us drinks and sat down. The conversation was severely embarrassing to me:

"How was work?" Shannon.

"Fine, slow, the tourists are tapering."

"Yeah, what can you do?"

"So I hear you and our guy here had a little time this morning?"

"Yeah, I guess."

"He has a nice dick don't you think, kind of big?"

"Oh, that's not big, bigger than average maybe."

"Yeah, but nice."

"Eh."

I could have choked on my embarrassment. It felt like a wet blanket was being shoved down my throat. Like a child. Like my parents were talking about me at some dinner party after I got up from sleeping to get a glass of water. I was so hyperaware that I wanted to run into the hills or jump in a ditch. But because I was a teenager, I said nothing.

The next two hours became a drunken blur, but we did make a plan to maybe take a road trip to Nevada and visit Mary's sister. She even got on the phone and called her. She said it was fine come out! She had just had a kid. She wanted her little sister to come see her niece.

We ended up dancing in the living room until her friend left. We egged her on as she crossed the street. Smoking cigarettes under the streetlight, the only sound was a cloud drifting across the moon. The noise was its shadow.

We laughed ourselves silly and ran around the house. The dogs barked and we told them to shush. It wasn't long before we gave up our selves. Or I think.

I woke up half dressed and half on and half off of the couch. My shoes were off, but my jeans were down past my butt. My face was grinding into the carpet, and my mouth tasted like quinine.

I think I had my first hangover.

I got up and went into the kitchen making my pants right. I drank so much water that I had to stop thinking for a second. When I started thinking again, I nearly threw up. The night came back to me and I decided I had had a good time. I poured a glass of water for Mary and went into her bedroom. She smiled at me and took a drink. She handed it back to me. I put the glass on the nightstand and got into bed next to her. I didn't take off my pants. I laid on top of the blanket she was under. She snuggled into me, her ass into my crotch. I didn't know what I was, but I think I was happy. I fell back asleep easy. And found no dreams.

Around noon I woke up eating a piece of nascent shaver cheese. My mouth was as dry as an unattended dairy kettle, scorched and soundless. I made motions with my mouth to generate saliva, to aggravate my scuttled cud. Mary was no longer in bed with me. I was sprawled out. I lifted my head to get a sense of my surroundings and turned my neck. I put my head back down. I saw the glass of water sitting on the nightstand. I sat up. I took a drink. The water was cool and clean. As it slid over my tongue and down my throat I could feel every inch of my body waiting for it. Sucking at it. My skin, my toes, and mostly my muscles. I drank the entire glass and stood up to get some more.

Mary was in the kitchen making coffee. Her hair was

in some weird hive on her head from sleep. She told me I looked the sight. I said I could say the same. She didn't smile and I slid by her to get more water.

I filled the glass with water twice and drank them both. I felt immensely better. I immediately had to use the bathroom. I spent the whole time worried she would come and knock on the door and try to come in. She didn't, but it was very unsatisfying. I flushed and brushed my teeth. I decided I needed a shower. I took one. This time it didn't burn my body because I knew the way the faucets worked. I was as clean as Sunday when I put my dirty clothes back on. I realized I should do my laundry.

When I went back to the kitchen she was pouring coffee. She said:

"Assume you want some?"

"Probably," she pressed against me as came over to the other counter where the cups were.

Jesus, you stink like a donkey. Give me your clothes, I'll wash them. I stood there like a donkey. Seriously, take em off. I took off all my clothes. And the rest, where are the rest?

I went and found my bag. I brought it to her. She was putting my dirty clothes in the washer that was next to the bathroom. She told me to dump it in. I dumped the rest of my dirty clothes into the hole. It smells like dirty boy, she said as she dumped detergent into the washer basin. She turned a bunch of knobs that I didn't understand. I stood there naked. I tried to kiss her. She pushed past me and went back into the kitchen and grabbed her coffee. I am taking a shower, she said and went around the other side of the kitchen, disappearing.

❦

I stood there naked for a moment, fully erect, the sound of the washer pouring water. I didn't feel thwarted, but I definitely felt exposed. I walked over and took my coffee from the counter and walked out onto the back porch. There was nobody around. I sat down and looked at the cliff and the dogs. I lit a cigarette. I was amusing myself with thoughts of whether or not anybody would care if I ever went back to W, specifically my mom and dad, when I heard Mary say from behind me, hey! I turned around in my seat. She was standing naked and dripping. She was moving her hands in a way that meant I should come join her. But really fast, like it was urgent. I ran in, of course, and found her naked and spread out on the bed. I was naked too, and could have broken vases with my erect dick, but we didn't have sex. It was almost parental guidance aside from the orgasms.

Afterward I went back out to the back porch and kept thinking my thoughts. I found the idea of going to Nevada so exciting that it was changing the way I was thinking. I didn't know if it would happen, but I wanted it to happen. I already had a narrative in my head.

Two older girls take a young hot dude on the road. The adventures!

The thing though is, that aside from a slight trip I took into Montana with my dad, with my two younger brothers when I was nine or ten, I had never left the state of Wyoming. I didn't have any clue what was out there. It could be anything.

I sat on the back porch smoking a cigarette, naked, when the washer made a noise that said it was done. I heard Mary go and throw the clothes into the dryer and hit a button that sounded like starting a car. The next noise was a clunk and then the sound of what could have easily been a clown rolling around in a rodeo barrel. I didn't give it much thought until she came onto the back porch wearing a summer dress and smiling like the Freon valves from a cooling tank. She said:

"You want me to call your mom?" She sat down.

"I don't know, think it will help?" I said. She lit a cigarette.

"Prolly, you're about as convincing as a shit-stain on a kite."

"How would your mom feel?"

"My mom is dead, don't think she'd feel anything."

"Ok, your dad?"

"I am calling her."

Mary spent the next ten minutes on the phone. When she was done she handed me the phone. I said:

"Mom?"

"Hi honey, how are you?"

"I'm ok."

"You can go with these girls if you want to."

"I think I want to."

"Ok, then listen to them, and wear your seat belt, you are precious cargo."

"Ok mom."

"I put your check in the bank."

"Ok, thanks mom."

"Do you have enough clothes honey?"

"I think so."

"Do you have a coat?"

"Mary said her dad could loan me one."

"Ok sweety, call me as much as you can."

"I will mom."

"I love you."

"Love you too."

I hung up and smiled. Mary looked me in the eye and decided to kiss me. The kiss was unexpected and my dick played with the air like a fencer. We were going to Nevada. And I had permission.

❧

When my clothes were dry a buzzer sounded. I went to the dryer and opened it. I put my jeans on. The button fly burned my dick a little. I wadded the rest of my clothes into my arms and kicked the door shut. I dropped a sock and when I bent down to pick it up the rest of my clothes spilled onto the linoleum. I wadded them up again. This time I held them so tightly my shoulder popped. It didn't help though. I lost two more socks on my way to Mary's bedroom. I threw the clothes on the bed and went back and picked up the socks.

When I got back to the bedroom I sat on the bed and put the two socks on my feet. I put on a t-shirt that said, "Work is a four letter word," it had a picture of a bear shrugging its shoulders. My aunt had sent it to me for Christmas. She lived in Montana on the Canadian border. I didn't know if the shirt was a joke or not, to her. I am guessing it wasn't, but she was my father's sister, so who knows. He wore shirts like that too, but out of necessity only. I believe. I mean, he would dress up sometimes and when he did he had some pretty fancy shirts to wear, and a beautiful pair of cowboy boots. But for the most part he only wore t-shirts and jeans. And because he had five boys we all shared the same jeans. The jeans that fit him. Thirty-six by thirty-six. They were too big for all of us. My younger brothers still had their kid pants, but me and my two older brothers only had these. We always had to wear a belt, and the jeans bunched up in the front and sagged in the back. The effect was comic, but we didn't know any different, so we rolled easily with it.

I crammed the rest of my clothes into my bag. I didn't bother folding anything because it didn't occur to me to do so. And the idea of pairing my socks made me uneasy for some reason. I couldn't stand the thought of my socks getting stretched out. When the elastic wore out on socks we called them, "quitters," and to me, the thought of a sock not staying up was worse than terrible.

I went into the living room and found my shoes. I sat on the couch and put them on. Mary came in while I was doing this. She said:

"What you think, we go today?"

"You call Shannon?"

"Yeah, she is down."

"How long is the drive?"

"Fourteen hours or so."

"Maybe we should leave tomorrow, ya think?"

"Yeah, prolly."

"I mean, what do we need to do to get ready?"

"Nothing really, get gas, maybe pack a tent and bags, groceries?"

"Fuck it."

"And anything you need to get in W?"

"Oh, I just need to go to the bank."

"Well it's settled then. Let's drink!"

We were excited. We spent the afternoon drinking beer and dancing. Her friend came over and we made plans. We would leave at seven and be there by eleven. We would take highway 20 to 26 to 287 and get on the interstate in Rawlins, and then follow the interstate through Salt Lake City and into Reno, then drop down into Carson City.

The morning was groggy. We had packed the car the night before. We had a cooler filled with things to make sandwiches. A tent and sleeping bags. Mary and I were smoking a cigarette and drinking a cup of coffee when her friend showed up carrying a bag of things and a sleeping bag. She opened the hatch on the car and threw her stuff inside. She slammed the hatch and asked us if we were ready. Mary took our coffee mugs inside and came back out. She locked the door. I had never seen anybody lock a door in Wyoming. I said:

"Locking the door?"

"Yeah, my dad might not be around for days."

"And what about the dogs?"

"They're fine. I called the neighbors."

"Oh, ok."

"Ready?"

We got in the car. I sat in the back. We stopped and got gas. The early morning sunlight cast red shadows over everything. The gas station was busy with work trucks, but we didn't have to wait. There was a line for the diesel pump though. I got out and washed the windshield as Mary pumped the gas. She went inside and paid and came back out holding three packs of cigarettes. We got back in the car and left.

The highway was swarming with deer and antelope. We had to swerve a few times to avoid hitting them. The sun was coming up over the hills to our left. We passed countless pastures fencing in cows and horses and sheep. Our windows were rolled down. The air smelled like manure and sagebrush. The sound of the air rushing past the car was deafening but liberating. I leaned back and closed my eyes. Thirty miles to W, stop and get some money, then freedom.

The next thirty minutes couldn't go quick enough. I had seen that stretch of road so many times I knew it by heart. The weird geodesic house on the hill right before South Flat. The drop into the valley by the Friedley's house. The Whitlock farm. The viaduct that spanned the Bighorn River. The gasworks and the turn-off to Washakie Ten. When we passed the A&W we were finally in town. We took a right at the IGA and drove two blocks. We pulled into the bank parking lot. I got out.

I went inside and filled out a form for withdrawal. I took it over to the teller and said hi. She knew me by name and asked how my parents were. I told her they were good and asked how she was. She said she was fine, but was nursing a sick pig and it was taking up all her time. I said that was too bad. She said, what can you do, he was scheduled for slaughter this weekend anyway, I don't even know why I bother. She gave me my money and told me to have a good one. I said thanks and went back to the car.

When I got in Mary and Shannon were smoking cigarettes and listening to the radio. Mary said, good to go? I nodded. She was looking at me from the rearview mirror. We pulled out of the parking lot and turned left. We took a right on Main. Main turned into Highway 20. Five minutes later we were past the city limits. I lit a cigarette. The feeling of freedom overwhelmed me. I felt giddy as we drove by the Boy's Home. I had a sense of accomplishment boiling like water on the top of my brain, and all I had to do was just sit there in the back seat and wait. I couldn't stop smiling. When we passed Gooseberry I knew I was free. I rolled up my window and put my head against the glass.

I woke up when we got to the canyon. Traffic was at a stand still. Before long we understood why. A boulder had fallen onto the highway. There was a truck turned over. Luckily nobody got killed, but the scene was grizzly. The man who was driving the truck stood staring at his vehicle in what looked like a state of shock. He was talking, or appeared to be talking to a highway patrolman.

It looked more like listening. A man in a yellow shirt was directing traffic. He wasn't a cop, or if he was a cop, he wasn't in uniform. We crept slowly past the accident. We all had rubbernecks. I rolled my window down. I could hear the river roaring and it smelled of Indian paintbrush. I felt a little panicky. I hated shit like this. This constant reminder that life was delicate. We got past the accident just as the ambulance and fire truck showed up. The rest of the ride through the canyon was white-knuckle for me even though we were driving well below the speed limit.

When we got to the tunnels Mary honked the horn through all three of them. We passed the dam and I told them about jumping off of it a couple weeks ago. They were impressed. They didn't believe me.

Past the dam the highway opened up onto an expanse of rolling hills and water. The reservoir was on the right. There were boats and people fishing. On the left the earth roiled into a beauty of dirty infinity. Herds of antelope grazing and pockmarked land broken up by ancient barbed wire fences with decaying wooden posts sun-grayed and askew. The mountains in the distance made the scenery sadly mystic. I felt inept in its majesty. It made me crave people. I was glad when we pulled into Shoshoni and took a right onto Highway 26.

The next two hours were kind of brutal, Riverton, Lander, Muddy Gap, the same old stupid landscape over and over. We smoked cigarette after cigarette and listened to the same cassette tape again and again. It wasn't until we hit the Interstate that the mood changed from boredom back to excitement.

We went from the standard yellow 55 mph road signs that mitigated the Wyoming highways to something new and white and faster. It was almost cosmopolitan. The new signs said we could do 70 mph. That was a terrifying prospect for a Toyota Tercel. We shook like a box of raisins and topped out at 65. We had to hug the right lane. Cars honked as they passed us.

The next four hours were more of the same old shit. I tried to stay awake but the boredom overtook me. The landscape didn't change, not once, and the only real difference was the change in the position of the sun. But nobody noticed that unless it was either in your eyes or burning your arm. We were driving so fast that smoking became a hassle. You couldn't roll your window down. We were drifting into a malaise until we got to the canyon just outside of Salt Lake City. We had to slow down again, and the landscape changed from drifting mounds of dirt to an element of danger.

It was cold outside, but we rolled the windows down anyway. We could smoke again, so we did. We talked about what we might do when we got to the city. We decided to check out the Tabernacle. We found it fascinating that we wouldn't be allowed to go inside because we weren't Mormon. We thought maybe we could find a way.

As we dropped down into the city from the canyon I couldn't believe it. So many people! So many houses! And all of it surrounded by mountains. It was beautiful. I had never seen a city before. I was jolted. I took off my seatbelt and leaned in between the front seats. My knees were shaking. I chain-smoked cigarettes and tried to be cool, but I wasn't cool. Everything was new and different.

We saw dogs on leashes. A leash! Nobody used leashes in Wyoming. And a guy selling hotdogs on a corner. Somebody with a sign asking for money. I was in the thick of it.

We had some trouble finding the church. Our map was outdated. We almost gave up. But then there it was. We parked and had to put money in the meter. This was also so incredibly new to me that I stared at the parking meter for twenty seconds before I could process it. Mary and Shannon were digging around in the car looking for things they thought that they needed. I fell in love with them, because what really could you need, I mean, we were just going around the corner. But I was also happy to just look at the parking meter.

After a minute or so they both were ready. Holding bags with god knows what. They slammed their doors and made sure they were locked. I went back and checked the door I came out of. It was locked.

The Tabernacle took up the entire block. It looked like a fortress. We had trouble finding the entrance. When we did find it, we tried to go in. There was a bouncer. He asked us if we were Mormon. For some reason we said no. He told us we couldn't go in. We stood there smoking a cigarette wondering what to do. Somebody decided we should eat something. I reminded them we had sandwich stuff in the car. Both their responses were: "Yeah, but we're in Salt Lake."

We walked a couple blocks and found a diner. The world was pedestrian in reality. But it vibrated like something electric. Every step I took was a step towards the future. The hostess that seated us looked like a Greek god. She might as well had been deciding my fate while telling us the soup was beef barley. The soup of the Gods.

I ordered a hamburger with fries. The girls ordered Ruebens. We talked about who would drive next. We still had eight hours to go. Maybe seven if we were lucky. I volunteered. But can you drive a stick? Who the hell doesn't know how to drive a stick? We finished our meals and drank as much coffee as we could stomach. We paid and took a piss before we left. Nobody broke into the car while we were gone.

❧

Mary handed me the keys. I opened the driver's side door and got into the driver's seat. I reached over and unlocked the passenger side door. Mary opened the door and reached behind and unlocked the back door. Shannon opened it and frumped into the back seat. The look on her face made me think her Rueben didn't sit well. Mary got in too and we all slammed our doors. I started the car and revved the engine. I didn't wait for the motor to idle on purpose, thinking it would be a funny joke to pretend I couldn't actually drive stick, I tried to put the gear shift into first. There was the sound of grinding. I looked over at the ladies and smiled. From the backseat I heard, Grind me a pound. We all laughed at this so hard that I accidentally put the car in third and lugged forward killing the engine. I got embarrassed as I pushed the clutch in and started the car, I put the car in first and released the clutch too fast while hitting the gas. The car peeled out. Mary said, Are you sure you can drive a stick? I told her to shut up. I was sure before, but now I wasn't so certain. Luckily I had other things to worry about.

It took us thirty minutes to get out of town. We got lost twice. It was a simple city, but I had never driven in a city. Neither had they in fact. Turns out this was the reason I was elected to drive, even though I was the worst driver. They didn't want to do it.

There were missed turns and merges that ended on side roads. At one point we ended up going into a canyon that we knew wasn't correct and had to pull off into a cul de sac to turn around. By the time we got back to the Interstate we were so relieved that we all lit cigarettes in celebration. We were back on the road. Mary put a tape in and nobody said a word. The sun was in front of us as the city disappeared in the distance. I put the sunscreen down to shield it from my eyes. I looked over and she was asleep. Her cigarette still burning in her hand. I shook her and she woke up. I told her to throw the cigarette out. She did. She rolled up her window. She leaned her head against it. She went right back to sleep. I craned my neck and looked into the back. Shannon was asleep too. Her window was rolled up. I could only assume her cigarette was gone.

The next few hours were marvelous. The girls slept as I maneuvered through the traffic on the Interstate. Mary had put the perfect tape in. Every time it finished one side, I just flipped it over and listened to the second. I rarely had to shift so I could light my own cigarettes, and the sun just slowly, and patiently, and decidedly, descended onto the edge of the earth. It felt like the Earth was moving, not us. Everything was blue for a while, then it went yellow, then red, then something else that combined all the three, then it went black. Before long the night became white again with stars. Then the moon started to rise. It was about then that Mary and Shannon both woke up.

"Where are we?"

"Somewhere in Nevada."

"Wow, fucking moon! How are we with gas?"

"Right! Quarter tank."

"I gotta piss," back seat.

"Ok, last sign said thirty, need me to pull over?"

"Yeah no, not that bad, god, how long have I been asleep? I dreamed that we were making beds for disabled widows from the Civil War and we couldn't quite get the corners right." She put her head between the two front seats. Her breath smelled like almonds.

"I don't know. Both of you fell asleep as soon as we left Salt Lake, four hours maybe? I listened to this album three times."

"Fuck, how long till we get there? This seat is itchy."

"Two hundred miles," I said.

"Fuck that. Wake me up when we pull over, I gotta piss." She disappeared into the back seat.

For the next thirty minutes Mary and I watched the moon rise over the Interstate. We both knew there was no future for us, I didn't want it, and she didn't want it, but there was an alacrity that made hanging out fun, and more than that, entertaining. We talked about things that nobody had ever talked to me about, things about my world view, how maybe the way I thought of things might make me jaded. How I should stay open to the world, choose a path based on my destiny. It was quite profound. Coming from somebody so much older than me. I took it all in.

When we pulled into the truck stop Shannon ran into the bathroom as we got gas. I cleaned the windshield. We had killed a ton of bugs. I had to wash it twice. When she got back she was smiling. She thought Mary should check it out. It was quite hilarious. She got back into the back seat and laid down.

I went in and paid. There were slot machines everywhere. Mary went into the bathroom. When I got back she was smiling. I said, what's that?, she said, oh nothing, just the bathroom has a glory hole! I couldn't resist, and found out the men's bathroom had one too. I peed even though I didn't need to. I bought a French tickler from the machine just for kicks.

When I got back to the car Mary said she would drive the rest of the way and didn't mind. I was ok with this. I was sick of driving and the florescent lights from the truck stops canopies made me feel delirious. The things I was looking at kept moving when I looked at them, like I was still on the road.

I asked:

"Why would a women's bathroom have a glory hole?"

"I don't know, renovations?"

We got back into the car and pulled back onto the Interstate. I was asleep before we hit forty.

When we pulled into Carson City I woke up because we were slowing down. Mary said, We're here, wake up you goofs. She shifted down into fourth, then third, the town looked smaller than I thought it would. I mean, it had the name City, but I didn't care, we got to where we were headed. It took me a minute to shake off my sleep, but by the time we pulled into a gas station to use the phone, I was ready for whatever came next.

We all stood around the payphone smoking cigarettes while Mary dug around in her pockets for her sister's phone number. When she found it she dug around some more for a quarter. She didn't have one. I had used my last two buying the French tickler, and Shannon never had any in the first place. I handed Mary my cigarette and went inside to get change. The cashier was black. Aside from my neighbors when I was eleven, I had never seen a black person. And not once, a black man. I stared on accident. He must have known because he said:

"Glorious right? And in his own image. What can I do you for?"

"Sorry I, um, change for the phone?" I handed him a dollar.

"It's ok to look, I know I am a handsome guy. Here ya go." He smiled and I ran outside without saying thanks. I could hear him laughing as I ran out the door.

I handed Mary the quarters and she gave me my cigarette back. I took a drag and it was finished. She picked up the receiver and dropped a quarter in the slot. I flicked the butt into the parking lot. She dialed her sister's number. Shannon went back to the car and sat down inside. I think she was nervous. But I also thought about the Rueben.

Mary's sister answered. I stood leaned against the wall trying to not look racist. I thought about lighting another cigarette, but I was burned out. I was excited, but I needed some real sleep. I was hoping this would go well.

When her sister answered she said:

"We're here!" It was sing-song. Her sister must have said something nice because she smiled. She made a motion towards me that meant get a pen. I ran over to the car and found one in the glove box. I brought it back. She wrote on the back of the paper that the phone number was on. She kept saying, Uh-huh, uh-huh. Before she hung up she said, "Ok, see you in a sec." She hung up the phone. She looked at me, she held up the directions, she said, "Here we go!"

"Yeah, she happy we're here?"

"I don't know, she has two kids and she sounds a little drunk, but whatever, no turning back now!" She looked over at Shannon in the back of the car and shouted, "Yo, Shanny! Come help me." She looked at me without saying anything. I knew what she meant though. I was too young. She was getting booze and she needed help.

I called 1-800-HOT-BOYS while I waited for the girls to get alcohol. They came back with a case of beer and two bottles of gas station wine. I opened the hatch for them. They put it in and I slammed the door back down. Mary reached into her pocket, pulled out the directions. She handed them to me. I looked at them. It was two numbers and a bunch of descriptions of things. I got into the shotgun seat and Shannon the back, and Mary got into the drivers seat. We all slammed our doors at the same time which caused all of our ears to pop. We all looked at each other and laughed. We didn't realize we couldn't hear that well. All the sudden we were sound virtuosic! Like we could control the earth with our ears alone.

❧

Mary's sister lived outside of town. We needed to go North and then East. And then take a side road that led us past a barn with two weather vanes and a cow farm with a yellow electric fence, if we got to the fork in the road we had gone too far. Her house was just down the gully and up and around the gigantic moss catcher.

We drank beer as we followed these directions. The windows were rolled down. The desert heat was dissipating. The air was cool and smelled like rural discipline, lilac, cow shit and diesel. The houses we passed had their front porch lights on. The land was flat as far as I could tell, judging how the road was, it was almost midnight. The road dropped down and up again. We came to a fork in the road. We had gone too far. We had to turn around. The moss catcher was obvious when we came back. We turned on the road that ran next to it. It was a dirt road. When we got to the house two dogs came to meet us. They were friendly. We all got out and Mary knew the dogs by name. She petted them. They wagged their tails. I finished my beer and crushed it into a puck. I went to the back of the car and opened the hatch. I put the puck inside and grabbed the beer and wine.

I did this on purpose because I didn't know how to meet people, and I knew that if I had things in my hands I wouldn't have to hug anyone or shake anybody's hand. I had also seen Mary's sister coming out the front door. She had a huge grin on her face. She was happy to see her sister. I knew the feeling. I knew there would be hugs involved. Also, she squealed with delight:

"Holy shit, you idiots made it!" Her sister ran over and hugged her. She hugged her friend too. She didn't hug me because I was holding the beer and the wine. Mary said: This is Joe. I nodded hello. "Well fucking eh , nice to meet you! Come in, come in!

"How was the trip? Don't tell me, let's get inside. Sorry, dogs, not tonight." One of the dogs smelled my butt. "Oh, he likes you! Come on! We'll get your shit later."

We went inside as the dogs whined. I got the impression the dogs were allowed inside sometimes, but they were young dogs, and probably pissed themselves with excitement. I guess it wasn't really an impression, but more of an observation, but I was high as a sponge and nothing was as straightforward as it seemed. I was taking everything in with the intention of processing it later.

The house was a ranch house. An actual ranch house. The layout was an open room with two bedrooms in the back. The living room was the kitchen was the dining room, and the only thing that separated them was couches or islands. Mary's brother in law was standing behind the island that made the kitchen. He came around and hugged both the girls. I put the booze on the marble counter and shook his hand. We exchanged names and I took a beer from the case and opened it. I was red in the face. I kicked a dog toy and said, whoops. He said don't worry about it. Those stupid dogs, if we don't give them something to chew on they eat the furniture.

I looked around. All the furniture had been chewed on. The place was cozy though. The lighting was yellow, and it smelled like pot roast. It reminded me of the Decker house on the hill, out by the lumberyard. I thought that if I went into the garage I would find a case of cheap soda.

The night didn't evolve to too much. Mary's friend got tired immediately and laid down on the couch and went to sleep. I tried to talk to her brother-in-law, but he was thirty and working in finance and I was sixteen on a road trip with his wife's sister. He got tired early too, and went to bed. He kissed his wife's cheek and hit the sack.

I tried to stay up. Mary and her sister were talking a mile a minute about Greybull and her plans to go to the University in the fall, and how their dad was doing. They both had the same voice. I got lulled to sleep. I don't remember falling asleep, but I was under the dining room table with a blanket on me when I woke up. I got up because I had to piss.

I found the bathroom easy. I peed and wanted to brush my teeth, but my bag was in the car. I instead went into the kitchen and drank from the faucet. Mary's sister had left lights on so we could find our way. I took the blanket from under the kitchen table and laid down next to Mary who was lying down next to her friend lying on the couch. I tried to snuggle up to her, but she rolled away. I had a sense that this might be the end to us, but I was still horny. I tried again, but this time she made a noise, a derision. I rolled away and went to sleep.

In the morning we were attacked by two kids, one four and one six. They were girls. They were hilarious and excited to have company. There was a lot of screaming. Mary played with her nieces and her friend complained. Complained about her lack of sleep, about how her head hurt, and the couch. I really couldn't understand why Mary was friends with her. She really was a stick in the mud.

There was coffee brewing. I could smell it. And pancakes. And bacon. I felt great and excited. I stood up and said a big hello. I went outside to get my stuff. The dogs rushed in. They immediately pissed on the floor. I said I was sorry. I should have known. They said don't worry about it, fucking dogs. I tried to help clean up, but Mary's sister told me to get lost. There were towels in the bathroom.

I took a shower and masturbated. Mary's sister was a curvy version of herself. I masturbated twice knowing I wouldn't have a second chance. I could have gone for a third time, but somebody knocked on the door and I had to yell I would be right out.

I brushed my teeth and put my clothes back on. I took my bag with me to the couch and put on clean socks. I felt alert and hungry. I put my shoes on and went to the island in the kitchen and sat down on a stool. I was given a cup of coffee. I said thanks. Mary was wrestling the kids in the living room and her friend was reading a book. I said:

"So what the hell, you guys like living here?"

"It ain't the worst, better than Greybull."

"Ha! Nobody likes Greybull, can't believe you guys grew up there."

"Yeah, Steve's never been there."

"Don't go."

"I hear it's a turd in a sea of turds." He smiled, I liked him.

"Worse than that."

"Here, eat this pancake, there is syrup over there."

"Thanks."

I ate pancakes and bacon until I was full. Mary played with her nieces until they got hungry. They came to the kitchen island and screamed, I want pancakes. I laughed. She sat down next to me and only drank coffee. She was pissed at me for trying to make a move on her the night before. I didn't know how to read it, so I let it go, but I didn't know what the problem was. I wasn't her boyfriend, and she definitely wasn't my girlfriend.

Something was coming down the pike. I knew it and she knew it, but the reckoning was as slippery as an elbow in a paper handshake.

♦

We spent half the day just hanging out at the house. I got bored first because I was the youngest. But I didn't say anything. Mary's frumpy friend got bored next and said as much. I'm bored, she said, let's go do something.

We consulted Mary's sister. She told us to go to Incline Village, Lake Tahoe. We could get lunch and maybe swim. Everybody liked this idea. We were on the road in minutes.

The drive up was beautiful. The lake was surrounded by trees. At one point we drove by a nude beach. We all craned our necks and joked about going there. Nobody saw anybody nude. When we got to Incline Village we had trouble parking until we realized it was a free-for-all. We parked on top of a rock, right next to a boulder.

The history of the town was funny. It was a mining town turned into a gambling town that turned into ghost town that turned into a tourist town. There was gambling still, but it was mostly souvenir shops that sold fake gold, and cafes with names like, Hard Luck Café, and, The Bottom Scraper. We went into the Bottom Scraper for lunch.

The restaurant had barrels for bar stools. The staff all wore hats. Prospecting hats. Which meant floppy cowboy hats. You could tell they didn't mind. They probably made three hundred dollars a day and got drunk at night and fucked each other. It felt like Cody, Wyoming, but with more money being exchanged.

We had to wait for a table. The place was busy. There were Elk heads on the wall that would have made my dad cringe. This made me smile. I loved my dad, but fuck that asshole. Who raises a teen in Wyoming? Especially when he knew better? I mean, he left his home in Montana to come to Wyoming to do what? The same thing over again? I don't know how it is possible to rebel against taxidermy, but I did it. I think I played a weird guitar lick in my head and frowned. I'll show him, I thought.

A minute or two went by. We were seated. It was a fun environment. The waiter came over and we ordered drinks. I got a root beer. The girls got bloody Marys.

He brought the drinks and took our orders. I got the Beef Dip with cheese and Mary and Shannon got the Ruebens again. I think they decided to see what a Rueben meant locally while traveling without telling me. That, or they really liked Ruebens. I didn't judge them. It was a tasty sandwich.

I nursed my root beer because it was artisanal and gross. The girls sucked the bloody Marys down. We didn't talk about much. The sandwiches came pretty quick. Mine was excellent. The girls both had to use the bathroom right after eating theirs. Whether it was from the bloody Marys or the Ruebens is beyond me, but whatever it was it didn't sit right.

I sat alone at the table trying to not imagine what noises they were making. This made things worse. I decided to step out for a smoke. I was standing on the wooden steps that made up the porch when they joined me. They had already paid. I said thanks and tried to give them money. They told me I got the next one. We agreed. I couldn't stop thinking about them having diarrhea so I forced myself to think about something else. It didn't work. All I could look at was their butts as we walked to the car. This wasn't the worst thing. Instinctively I needed to break away from these two. They were awesome, but bad news.

We got back in the car and decided that when we got back to Mary's sisters house we would pack our shit back up and head to Reno. Probably spend the night in the back of the car and go to San Francisco the next day.

❧

When we got back to her sister's house it was early afternoon. We got our stuff and told her we would see her on the way back through town. She didn't seem to mind. She looked a little hungover. She almost seemed angry because of it. This made her more sexy to me. There were a few minutes to spare as the girls packed up their things. I went into the bathroom. I felt better when I came back out.

We packed the car and gave hugs. The dogs and the kids and the husband were nowhere to be seen. There was a barking and the sound of a motor off in the distance. I assumed that was them. I didn't want to hug Mary's sister but she made me. Touching her went straight to my bones. I frowned. I ran and jumped into the back seat in order to hide my boner.

The girls got into the front seats. We pealed out in the driveway on accident. The dogs must have heard this because they came running from wherever they were. They barked us onto the road. I rolled down my window and stuck my head out. I yelled at them. You're like a tree, man, quit barking! They followed us for a quarter mile then gave up.

We had to go through town and get back on the Interstate. We drove for an hour or so before we saw a sign for Sparks, Nevada. Then there was another sign that said: Reno, so close to hell you can see Sparks.

Then Reno.

Reno was a small town, but also a big city. There were casinos and a Main street. We pulled over at a mall and parked. We went into the music store and bought some cassettes. We had all sorts of new music when we came out. I don't remember ever being so happy. We couldn't get this music in Wyoming. The first tape, whatever it was, didn't matter, the idea, though, blew my mind.

It was on full blast as we cruised the Strip.

We looked for an all ages club that we couldn't find and eventually ended up parking on a side street. We got out and decided to walk around. At some point the girls got antsy and decided we should go into a casino. I tried to follow them in, but I was too young, so they laughed and ran away inside leaving me on the street.

I couldn't blame them. Four years is a long time between 16 and 21. And I really didn't mind. I walked back and forth on the Strip and smoked cigarettes. At one point I ended up hanging out with a Vietnam veteran who had a cardboard sign that said:

I'm Vet. Need Money. Yes.

He was hilarious and I talked to him until the girls came out of the casino, drunk and giggly. I said goodbye to the veteran and gave him a twenty. I led the girls to the car. I drove us to a gas station on the edge of town to sleep at. They were both asleep when we got there. I was able to put one of the back seats down without waking anybody. I got comfortable pretty easy. It wasn't long before I fell asleep.

The heat was stifling in the car when I woke up. I was so sweaty I nearly puked. Both the girls had already got up and left the car. They were drinking cups of coffee and staring at a map they had laid out on the hood. I wrangled myself from the sleeping bag I had tangled myself into and pushed the door open. I pushed my legs through and stood up. The concrete was hot on my socked feet. I stretched and walked to the front of the car. Mary looked down at my feet. She said, What are you a millionaire? Making reference to the fact that I was just wearing socks and I shouldn't be walking in them on the concrete because I would put holes in them. This shamed me enough to go to the back and lift the hatch and put my shoes on.

When I got back they had folded up the map and were smoking cigarettes. One of them handed me a coffee. The coffee was cold and I drank it in one continuous drink. I felt better and awake. I took their empty coffee cups and took the lids off and stacked them inside each other. I stacked the lids on top too. I took them to the trashcan nearest to us. I said I had to pee. I went to the back of the car again and got my toothbrush and toothpaste. I went inside the gas station.

The bathroom was pretty gross and smelled like piss. I went to the bathroom and then washed my hands and my face. I brushed my teeth. I felt dirty not taking a shower only because I had slept in my clothes and was wearing the same socks as yesterday. But I was clean in the front and clean in the back, so I couldn't really complain.

There was a diner next door to the gas station called The Rapid Arm. We decided we should get some breakfast before heading out. The waitress who sat us asked if we wanted coffee. We all said yes. When she came back with the coffees I ordered the biscuits with gravy and the girls ordered breakfast burritos.

As we waited for the food I was informed that it would take about three and a half hours to get to San Francisco. That seemed like a short amount of time at this point. I was glad. I was sick of driving. As exciting as it was, travel was tedious. We decided to take the quickest route possible, which meant the Interstate.

The breakfasts came and mine was delicious. The girls had the same reaction to their burritos as they did to the Ruebens the day before. I started to wonder what was up. What was it? Choices or body? I decided at this moment to not ever order whatever they were ordering. Just in case.

We paid our bill and got back in the car. I got in the back. I had to police my things before doing so. The car was starting to smell. Like metal rubbing on hair combined with 3 in 1 oil mixed with a bad tooth. We all rolled the windows down to air it out.

When we got onto the Interstate again we had to roll the windows up. This was ok because we had new music to listen to. We were happy for about an hour and a half before we decided to pull over and have a picnic of wine and cigarettes.

We were in California at this point. We pulled off onto a parallel road and found a liquor store. The girls went inside and bought a bottle of Coconut Shandy thinking it would be funny. We drove about a mile down the road and the road started to run next to a cliff that was next to the ocean. We pulled over at a campsite/picnic area. We got out and walked to the edge of the cliff. The ocean was beautiful. The waves seemed like they were laughing at us, or trying to eat us, but we were on a cliff so they couldn't reach us.

We passed the Coconut Shandy around and it was terrible. It was warm and gross and I said as much. This sent Mary into some weird attack on me about how I was a loser and a jerk and I needed to get my shit together and nobody loved me because I was stupid and I should jump off the fucking cliff because nobody would give two goddamns.

She stormed off.

It was weird because I knew it wasn't directed at me specifically. But it still hurt my feelings. I was sixteen. Why was I being yelled at. I moped back to the car and sat in the back seat with the door open. I watched her storm off into some trees that were next to the cliff. I could see her kicking rocks and talking to herself. Her friend took the bottle of liquor and sat down at the picnic table and watched the ocean, taking swigs periodically.

Everything was beautiful except for the emotions. It was an hour before Mary came back. She got into the driver seat without saying a word. Her friend was drunk and stumbled into the car and then told us to wait. She pulled her pants down and pissed in full view. The wind wafted her crotch to me and I was rock hard immediately. It didn't help that I could see her vagina's lips undulating through her hairy piss soaked pubes. I didn't bother to look away. I had masturbation material for a month.

She stood up and pulled up her dirty panties. She zipped her jeans and got into the front seat. She slammed the door. I slammed my door too. Mary looked straight ahead. When the doors were closed she sped off onto the highway and flipped a U. Her friend turned the music up thank god. It killed the tension.

We got back on the Interstate. We only had an hour or so to go. Shannon passed out almost immediately. I kept an eye on Mary from the back seat. The rearview mirror was angled just right. Her eyes were angry for quite some time. Eventually she gave it up. About thirty minutes outside San Francisco she decide to try the radio. We picked up a local punk rock station. Things got exciting again. Her anger was gone. This was better than anything I had ever known. I mean, this was a city, an actual city. We were about to be there, and fuck all emotion, this shit was great!

The Golden Gate Bridge was kind of excellent. Huge-ass bridge. I kind of wanted Mary to pull over so I could jump over the edge for the sake of posterity. There were boats underneath, and traffic was stalled in the outgoing lanes. I barely noticed the city at all until we were in it.

We took a left when we got to the city proper. There was a park. We pulled into the lot on its edge and found a space. We got out taking the map with us. Our map was old. Mary's sister had given it to us before we left. It was wrong. It was five years old. We knew it was wrong because we shouldn't have been able to take a left at the end of the bridge. But here we were, standing where we were standing.

There was nothing to care about though. We knew where we were and we had no place to go. I stared at boats and the bridge as Mary and Shannon tried to make sense of the map they had laid out on the hood of the car.

I smoked a cigarette and felt liberated. The girls had furrowed brows. I smiled in my liberation. They frowned. I mean, the city was a lollypop at best, there was nowhere we could go without ending up at the entrance again. What was there to worry about? But because they had plans, they worried.

There were two places to go, or three if you count downtown, but that was just on the way.

We got back in the car and went downtown. We parked and took twenty minutes trying to figure out if we could park without paying a ticket. We couldn't. We walked around for a while and everything was super clean. Too clean for a city. There were No Smoking signs outside. Who can't smoke outside? That's some fucking weird ass shit. There were jugglers and performance artists, hippies handing out bills, and musicians playing covers of Dead songs. I loved it, but I was alone in this thought. We went immediately back to the car.

The next stop was up and over the hill. There was a wharf that looked onto the prison. It smelled nice. We ate some lunch and decided to get a hotel room.

In order to get to where we thought we should go we followed a road around the edge of the city. Every single street was a one-way against us. It was funny at first, but by the time we ended up back where we started in the first place there were no longer any happy feelings.

We dipped up and down and then up again and took a weird wild left that took us down a very, very bendy street that seemed improbable, that should have rolled the car, but because the street was made of asphalt, there was grip, and we made it to the bottom without incident.

We ended up in Chinatown.

We parked easy. There was a hotel with a sign that said: Hotel. Mary put the emergency brake on. We were parked on a hill. When I opened the door it smelled like garlic. It was late enough we didn't need to put money in the parking meter.

The sun was down and everybody was burnt.

It was a strange moment of insight that kept me from going inside the hotel lobby. I don't know why I knew better, but I knew better. The girls went inside and procured a room. When they came out they said that there could be only two people to a room and I should go hide for a moment. One of them would come find me after they checked in.

The door to the hotel was different than the door to the lobby. The girls disappeared upstairs. When they came back down I was standing next to the car. We gathered our luggage and took it through the door and up the stairs to the second floor. The room was puny. It had a double bed and a bathroom. And a window that looked out on the street. We talked briefly about maybe having me sleep in the car just in case, but then we decided, fuck them, we just gave them fifty bucks.

Things were exciting but we didn't know what to do. We thought we might should do something, but what we did not know. We smoked some pot. Not long after we were stoned.

Shannon got so stoned she freaked out and hid under the covers of the bed. Mary and I laughed about this. We decided we should go for a walk. Went downstairs with every intention of going out into the city.

We didn't make it very far. Our eyelids were as heavy as sandbags and our sense of direction disappeared the moment we got two blocks away. And Chinatown was as crazy with action as it was with smells. Both of us were too scared and too stoned to explore much further. We laughed about this and headed back to the room.

We accidentally went into the lobby on our way back. The Asian woman glared at us and said:

"He's not in your room right!"

"Oh, god no! Just some perv from the street."

"Better be!"

We backed up outside and went in through the right door. We laughed all the way to the room. We were certain the lady at the counter knew what we were up to, but didn't care. She just needed to say something. Shannon was asleep when we got inside. She looked peaceful. Mary took her shoes off and got in bed with her. I asked her for the keys and went down to the car and got my sleeping bag and my bag.

When I got back they were both asleep. I went into the bathroom and locked the door. I masturbated to the thought of the woman at the front desk coming up and busting through the door and finding us all naked lying on the bed and then the three girls sucking my dick in unison.

I cleaned up and brushed my teeth. I unlocked the door and laid my sleeping bag on the carpet. I was asleep even before I closed my eyes.

❧

In the morning we checked out early. I hid by the car as the girls dealt with the front desk. The normal day-to-day pace of the city made me dizzy. I chain-smoked cigarettes and tried to look cool, but nobody gave a shit. This was Chinatown San Francisco.

The girls ran to the car when they came out of the office. They said it worked and nobody knew we had three people in the room. This was good. We got in the car and decided to go south. We got lost a couple times and had to go down streets we didn't want to, but in the end we ended up on the Interstate cranky and annoyed and hungry and thirsty for coffee.

Somewhere outside of the city we stopped at a diner. We parked and went inside. The place had a Mexican theme happening. We all ordered the huevos rancheros with coffee. The food was quite excellent. We talked about the plan. We looked at the map. Santa Cruz was only ninety miles away and there was a beach there and a boardwalk with a Ferris wheel and other rides. It seemed the most logical.

We paid and got back in the car.

The hour and a half of driving was supposed to be exciting but it wasn't. Being from Wyoming the ocean didn't have that much appeal to any of us. The radio was boring when it shouldn't have been, and the landscape never really changed.

When we got to Santa Cruz we cruised around a little and found the boardwalk with the Ferris wheel. We parked and got out. We walked around for a while and nobody really cared to go on the rides. I bought a hotdog from a vender just to make the moment somewhat memorable. The hotdog was lukewarm and made me a little sick. There was talk of going further south, down to Los Angeles, but we all decided we had seen enough of California. We decided we should just head back. I was still exited and would have easily stayed on the road, but I was also sick of the girls and their consistent bad attitudes. And they were sick of me, and my childish nature. If there was a way to split ways at this moment we would have, but we were all stuck in the same car, with more or less the same destination.

We got back in the car. We discussed whether we should drive back to Mary's sisters house before we headed back home. Home was an eighteen-hour drive, but there was three of us, if we each took a six hour shift we could just do it straight. This seemed reasonable so we nixed her sister's house and got back on the Interstate.

The first gas station that came along we pulled into to fill up the gas tank and get road things. I bought jerky and a coffee. I would be the first to drive. The girls bought water and granola. Mary bought a banana, she used it as a telephone at the counter. We all laughed, including the cashier. Stupidity is universal. Nobody had to piss so we got right on the road.

Driving through California was nice, but when we hit Nevada it became a little brutal. It's one thing for things to be pretty, it's another for them to be beautiful and unchanging. I could have slept in the arms of the desert. I didn't bother with music. I let my head gather all the thoughts it had repressed since leaving W. I was a changed person. I saw something new, something new about the world that I didn't know existed. There were things out there! Things for me to see, things that weren't just growing up in Wyoming and dealing with big fat jerks. I don't know, it was a nice feeling, like playing tetherball, but then the ball snaps off from the rope and ends up in the thorn patch and you go get it and all the sudden you have thorns stuck to the bottom of your shoes and when you get back on the pavement of the playground your shoes make a different sound. And you try to knock them off, but they won't knock off, and you don't care because recess is over and you have to run back inside.

I drove and drove and drove. The girls slept. When we got close to running out of gas I pulled into a truck stop. I got out and filled the tank and washed the windshield. The girls didn't wake up. I was ok with this. I decided to keep driving.

It wasn't long until we were back in Utah. The sun was going down. I was eating jerky and thinking wonderful thoughts. Mary woke up. She had been asleep for nearly eight hours. She asked me, where the fuck are we? Somewhere in Utah. How long I been asleep? Nearly eight hours. Shit. Need me to drive? Probably.

We pulled over on a truck break check before we hit the mountains. I got out and peed. Both the girls did too. The air was cold. We all shivered when we got back in. I got in the back seat. Shannon decided to drive. I told them there was jerky if they wanted. I leaned my head against the window and looked up at the stars. I fell asleep before we were doing cruising speed. The radio came on, but I barely noticed, Mary adjusted the sound to the front of the car. They were laughing and eating jerky as I drifted out.

When I woke up we were in Wyoming. Apparently I had slept through Salt Lake and all of the mountains. It was well past dawn. Nearly eleven. I asked them where we were. They said outside Kemmerer. Oh, shit, need me to drive? Maybe, how you feeling? Pretty good, hungry though. Ok, twenty-three miles to a pull off. You guys eat all the jerky? I took my seatbelt off and lunged between the seats. All gone. Damn it! I got back into the back seat and put my seatbelt back on. Twenty-three miles of hunger.

When we pulled into the gas station I got out to stretch my legs. Mary washed the windshield as Shannon went to the bathroom. I went inside and looked around for something to eat. I found a burrito to microwave. I spent a minute and a half making sure it would get so hot that it burned my hands when I took it out. I held it by its plastic skin as I took it to the front counter. The woman didn't touch the burrito. She knew it was too hot. She glared at me for not buying it before putting it in the microwave. I said I was sorry, but I wasn't really sorry. I got into the driver's seat and waited as Shannon came back to the car after going to the bathroom and then Mary went to the bathroom herself.

We were on the road right after, and both the girls fell asleep. I drove until five in the evening before anyone woke up. We were pulling into Shoshoni. I was done driving. I said, wake up, someone else needs to drive, we are almost at the canyon. Oh, shit really? Fuck. Pull over. K, we need gas anyway.

When we pulled into town I got into the turning lane and pulled into the gas station. I was burnt out and needed to piss. I went inside without talking to anybody.

Everybody got out to piss. Mary got a coffee because she was going to drive the last leg. I got a microwave burrito. They didn't have hot sauce so I got some mustard packets. We got back into the car. I got into the back seat. We pulled onto the highway and took a left. We forgot to get gas. Mary looked at the fuel gauge and decided we could make it to Thermopolis, it was all down hill anyway she reasoned. I said sorry, I had to pee. Not only that but I had been driving for eight hours straight.

The landscape looked the same as it did when we drove up the canyon, but in reverse. The reservoir was on the left and the endless hills and sagebrush to the right. I ate my burrito. The mustard was a good accent to the spicy beef.

I fell asleep before we got to the Canyon. I slept all the way through it. I briefly woke up in Thermopolis when we got gas, but was asleep again by the time we reached the sign that said Worlds Largest Hot Springs. I didn't wake up again until we were just outside of W. I was happy to be home. I was sick of traveling. When the hill with the giant W came into view I didn't hide my excitement. I asked the girls to turn up the radio.

We slowed down and dropped into town. The Annex was full of trucks getting gas. Mostly diesel. We crossed the Big Horn River and the movie theater. We crossed the train tracks and waited for the light. We cruised down Main. The bank sign said it was 6:17. We took a left at the City building with the weird statue of Chief Washakie and then a right on Robertson. Four blocks later we pulled in front of my house.

Well I guess this is you. We all got out and went to the back of the car. I opened the hatch and swung it up. I grabbed my shit and put it on the ground. I slammed the hatch back down. Nobody told me I shouldn't slam the fucking door. I suddenly regretted being back home, but it passed just as sudden.

I said goodbye and thanks to both of the girls. They

hugged me. Maybe you will come to Laramie? I knew the answer was yes, but I said ok anyway. I picked up my bag. They got back into the car and drove away. I watched them take a left two blocks down. I felt a little ache.

The gravity of the last couple weeks hit me as I crossed the street. I wanted to go with them, but not those two necessarily, just the idea. Summer was over and school would start again soon. I didn't want to go back to school. School was stupid and people were mean and I hated my teachers and my classes. Shop was alright because I knew how to run the lathe and Art was wonderful because of the teacher, and so too Math and German, but I felt like I really didn't belong.

What I had just seen was a world I had never knew or known existed. There was a world out there, a world I didn't know about that I needed to see. I made a promise with myself that I would do something with my life. The plan was vague and involved dropping out of school. I thought this as I climbed the concrete steps of my house.

I opened the door.